Life is a Tango

Alice Holeman

BALBOA.
PRESS

A DIVISION OF HAY HOUSE

Cover illustrated by the Author

Balboa Press books may be ordered through booksellers or by contacting:

Balboa Press
A Division of Hay House
1663 Liberty Drive
Bloomington, IN 47403
www.balboapress.com
1 (877) 407-4847

Because of the dynamic nature of the Internet, any web addresses or links contained in this book may have changed since publication and may no longer be valid. The views expressed in this work are solely those of the author and do not necessarily reflect the views of the publisher, and the publisher hereby disclaims any responsibility for them.

The author of this book does not dispense medical advice or prescribe the use of any technique as a form of treatment for physical, emotional, or medical problems without the advice of a physician, either directly or indirectly. The intent of the author is only to offer information of a general nature to help you in your quest for emotional and spiritual well-being. In the event you use any of the information in this book for yourself, which is your constitutional right, the author and the publisher assume no responsibility for your actions.

Any people depicted in stock imagery provided by Thinkstock are models, and such images are being used for illustrative purposes only. Certain stock imagery © Thinkstock.

Printed in the United States of America.

ISBN: 978-1-4525-2063-6 (sc)
ISBN: 978-1-4525-2065-0 (hc)
ISBN: 978-1-4525-2064-3 (e)

Library of Congress Control Number: 2014914702

Balboa Press rev. date: 10/03/2014

Contents

This book is dedicated to Doris Gates (Dori), my best friend and "surrogate" mother. She has been my North Star for years, during all our spiritual explorations and, most recently, while I worked on this book.

Author's Note

Although there is much diversity across spiritual traditions, I have long had the conviction that, at the core, all religions have much common ground. Each reaches for a connection to that ineffable "Source" of power and love. So, the presence of exclusivity, separation and violence between spiritual communities has always puzzled me.

Therefore, I was challenged to actually write about my belief. But to do so, I had to do some investigation to back up those convictions. Never having been a devout fan of religion, but rather an avid stalker of the ethereal *spirituality,* as I researched the subject, I was delighted to feel a growing admiration for each religious system—each one tailored for the special culture it serves.

I believe that stories and examples can often demonstrate truths better than dry facts. As my characters, mostly women of various religions, thread their way through their adventures, experiences and challenges, it serves to demonstrate the similarity of the One Spirit that hides just under the surface of what we think is reality.

I hope you enjoy the journey and the dance with Jo McRae.

Alice Holeman

Characters

Jo	- Christian Widow
Jack	- Tour Director
Sonya	- Hindu Friend
Medina	- Sufi Muslim Friend
Rachael	- Jewish Friend
Todd	- Buddhist Friend
Takil	- Buddhist-Taoist Friend
Mildred	- Fundamentalist Christian
Silver-haired Ladies	- Christians
Miguel	- Mayan Priest
John	- Native American
Rita	- Sexy Agnostic

*"The number one obstacle to interfaith is a
bad relation with one's own faith tradition"*

The Dalai Lama

———————————————

*"To everything there is a season, and a
time to every purpose under the heavens."*

Ecclesiastes 3:1

———————————————

*"God speaks to us in three places:
in scripture, in our deepest selves,
and in the voice of a stranger."*

Thomas Merton

———————————————

CHRISTIANITY "*To understand the world, knowledge is not enough. You must see it, touch it, live in its presence and drink the vital heat of existence in the very heart of reality.*"

Teilhard Chardin

---

1 Who Am I...? What Are We?

Jo McRae... Widow? Does that medieval label define me now?

A rumbling beneath the plane seat brought me back to the present, and to the shuffling, coughing and checking of seat belts all around. Soon the huge plane lumbered out onto the runway, then turned from an awkward creaking beast into a splendid, powerfully-made machine. It felt like a force of nature as it pinned me back into the seat. I silently prayed, *Into Your hands I commend my spirit...* just in case of calamity.

Turning to my seatmate after the landscape vanished outside, I smiled. I was embarking on a tour and I knew the woman next to me was also a member of the group. She fastened friendly dark eyes on me from above a small, vintage body of advanced years clothed in a flowing traditional Indian sari.

"Hi. I'm Jo McRae," I said. "We met earlier at the gathering of tour members, but there were too many names for my brain."

"Mine is Sonya Saguna," answered my seatmate, as she wiggled under her seatbelt with child-like anticipation. "I've been dying to see South America all my life. It's unbelievable to finally have that dream come true, with even a stop in Mexico to finish off the tour. I can't wait for the lectures sprinkled all through the trip on out-of-body experiences, near-death experiences and extra-terrestrial evidence with the Inca and Mayan ruins. To get this all in one package is a trip of a lifetime." Her enthusiasm was contagious.

I nodded, "I've seen our guide, Jack Zuko, on the television History Channel. Now we're going to actually *see* some of the places he talks about."

Thinking back to the group meeting a few hours earlier, our guide had seemed more attractive than on television, with a thick bodied, olive-skinned and silver-haired Mediterranean look about him. The tour, *Expand Your Horizons,* consisted of twenty people, appearing to be very culturally diverse.

Leaning across Sonya, I saw that the tour participants seemed to all be concentrated close to us, across the wide jet. We were grateful that we had two seats close to a window and not in the wide center section that contained several people in each row. Our tour group was an unusual bunch of folks and I tried to guess at their religions and countries of origin.

"Sonya, what religion are you?"

"I'm Hindu, but that is a reeeeeeally broad category with some attitudes and beliefs I don't personally hold," she said.

"I'm Christian, but I don't understand so much that passes as Christianity today. Actually, sometimes I'm embarrassed because it doesn't sound like Jesus to me." We seemed to have something in common with our ambivalent religious feelings.

As Sonya's eyes fastened on my face with such an open kindness, impulsive thoughts spilled right out of my mouth, unbidden. "This life we're given is so exhilarating... and so devastating. I'm hunting for the purpose—the reason."

What in the world made me pop out with that*, and to a perfect stranger?*

"Oh Jo... You have some important thoughts stewing in your mental cauldron! What's going on?" Not showing any surprise or judgment, Sonya just watched me and waited, smiling encouragingly.

"Well... I've always been enthusiastic about life. It's been filled with marriage, children and a rewarding nursing career." Grinning self-consciously I admitted, "I was an avid, *'rabid'* collector of landscaping plants to complete my rock and waterfall gardens. And it's been a passion of mine to read just about everything I could find on spirituality."

I stopped talking as I heard the plastic cap "pop" on a little airline liquor bottle. The smell of bourbon wafted up over my seat from a man who was about to enjoy a nightcap drink. For me, that smell was indelibly attached to heartache. Emotion choked back any further words.

Sonya's face and body bent forward toward me with complete attention as if to coax the words out of me.

I swallowed and continued, "Before my husband, Ron, died unexpectedly of a heart attack, the marriage had become a challenge. The handsome, self-assured architect I married eventually became disillusioned as the styles of houses and buildings changed into something he could not appreciate. There was no market for his beautiful, earthy, rock and cedar designs anymore, at least not in the city where we lived. His copious social drinking became more constant, although he dutifully continued to crank out architectural plans for which he had no passion.

"At night he drank to cope, and I became like a second wife. His companion… and comfort… was the bottle, not me. I fought for him. He agreed to rehab, dried out and then couldn't hold on to the sobriety. I planned trips—the bottle went along. I screamed and yelled, bought sexy underwear, drank with him. Nothing could get through.

"A man's self-worth can be so tied up with his vocation—his *work*—that his sense of self vanishes with the job. I think, to him, the ultimately fatal heart attack was a release from the misery.

"Through those lonely years, Al-Anon, the support organization for friends and families of alcoholics, saved my sanity. 'Sick in the head' myself, and exhausted, they nurtured me back to health. For the first time, I learned to *trust* my Higher Power, God—to turn over the controls of my train-wrecked life and *it actually worked!* Agonies subsided—problems solved themselves." Smiling, I told her of a sign on my mirror, my mantra. "Let Go or Be Dragged!"

"But when Ron died, everything fell apart. Our son did too—grabbed a bottle and vanished, himself.

"Three years later, I just can't get a grip back on life. All the legal, financial and social adjustments are done. I sold our house and gardens and passed our furniture and various belongings to our children because Ron was involved in every piece. The memories kept hurting too much. The kids and grandkids now come to see me at my apartment on a little lake surrounded by woods that God takes care of. Still, there's no zest, no joy. Darn it, I'm still here... for What?"

Sonya shrugged her little shoulders and said, "You're not done yet, Jo. There's a lot more life waiting for you."

"The key has to be spiritual. My church goes through the motions, the rituals—but, for me, it's all flat. There's no *experience* of God there. A yearning comes up in me, wanting to be answered again. But the connection is broken. My battery is dead, corroded.

"The magazine, Whole Spirit, looked interesting because it discusses other religions. There might be a spark for me there, by exploring the different faiths. This tour advertisement, in the magazine, seemed to jump off the page. I'm hoping to be around lots of people of different religions and to find out all about them, their beliefs. Maybe I don't need to be a Christian anymore."

Grinning at her and embarrassed, I willed her to understand. *What in the world made me unload all my troubles onto this perfect stranger—I **am** losing it!*

With a sweet affectionate grin, Sonya snuggled her shoulder next to mine and said, "I understand your dilemma and feel your pain. You've made a good choice to come on this tour. It's a start. I came because this sounded like a fantastic experience, and I don't want to miss anything, *anything* I can get out of life."

It was getting late—midnight already. We would fly all night to make the trip seem less tedious. The flight attendants had provided pillows and blankets for each of us and I tucked my pillow next to the window and settled under the blanket, just as Sonya seemed to want to do.

Sleep didn't come easily because our seats were near a bathroom and we were frequently serenaded with a "creeeeak/bang, creeeeak/bang" of the door as the disheveled and stiff passengers trudged back and forth through the night.

Out of frustration, both awake, we turned the seat lights on to read. Sonya retrieved a little laptop computer from her satchel under the seat and bent intently over it, completely absorbed.

After a while I asked, "What are you working on?"

"I'm attempting to write a book. My old journals have recorded the problems and obstacles that turned into blessings and I feel like there's some wisdom to be shared. When I journal, a voice comes to me through the pages and counsels me. My challenges turn into knowledge and wisdom gained." She humbly smiled. "I don't know if I'm good enough—if I can really pull it off."

"How *wonderful* Sonya," I whispered, trying not to wake the people fortunate enough to be asleep.

She said, "I have notes from my journal in one file and the book in another file in this computer. It's so wonderful, no heavy paper work to drag around!" She had mastered the new computer technology. Such a youthful, inquisitive spirit.

She shyly handed me the laptop and I began to read her book and… didn't want to stop reading. It was good! As I read on, she finally fell asleep. Later, I reluctantly turned off the light and fell asleep myself.

A sudden sickening drop of the plane shocked me awake and we seemed to *levitate,* thankfully restrained by the seatbelts. Everyone was rousing and looking around for some explanation.

Overhead lights came on and the pilot announced, "We have a bit of bad weather to pass through, so please stay in your seats with your seat belts buckled."

The heavy plane listed sideways and dropped again and then, whack! A sudden jolt to the side whipped my head hard into the window-frame before I could brace myself. Staring stupidly ahead, I tried to make sense of what had just happened.

Sonya grasped my arm and peered at my face. She exclaimed, "Your eyebrow is bleeding!" Quickly, a soft handkerchief was pulled from her pocket and pressed to my forehead while she called for someone to find a flight attendant.

I thought… *So, sari's have pockets. I didn't know that.*

A brave flight attendant came down the aisle, desperately clinging to each seat back as she passed. The handkerchief was replaced by a bandage and eventually I received some Tylenol for my growing headache.

The movements of the plane were unpredictable and slightly nauseating and we heard definite sounds of vomiting somewhere behind us. After a little while, the plane quieted its shuddering, the sudden drops in altitude, and all was smooth again.

Thoroughly shaken, I couldn't seem to get calm, still quivering inside.

Sonya noticed my discomfort and quietly collected our two pillows which she placed on her lap, and then after raising the arm rest between us and adjusting the seat-belts, she gently pulled my head and shoulder onto the pillows. Smoothing my sweaty hairline and separating the strands of hair softly and kindly, I found myself being gently mothered by a stranger. The previous shock and the emotion of it caused me to tear up and sob quietly. Sonya just kept stroking my forehead and hair and even hummed a little song under her breath. It calmed the trembling and I felt incredibly *loved.*

A little while later we straightened ourselves up, smiled at each other, and I said "Thank you, from the bottom of my heart."

"Speaking of your heart, precious Jo, it's been broken by the death of your husband. You've locked your heart away for safe keeping." Her eyes twinkled as she said, "It's got a cast-iron chastity belt around it; no feeling can get past those metal barriers. But it's nearly impossible to talk yourself out of it—you instinctively protect your damaged heart.

"Being a nurse, you think three years is long enough, but grief has no time limit. Compound that with all the guilt you've dumped on yourself for not 'getting a grip' and your ambivalent feelings about the marriage—what should have been, what could have been. Jo, you've been *brutal* to yourself. Would any patient of yours ever get that kind of treatment?"

I hung my head and admitted, "No, of course not."

Sonya continued, "My husband died too, five years ago. As a Hindu I know he's not gone, but 'just around the next corner'. Still, losing him was terribly painful to live through. It took a while, but eventually I decided to live each day as if it is my last and to enjoy life as much as possible.

"I suspect you have been a passionate woman your whole life, Jo. When you were chasing those desires, pursuing those special plants or incredible rocks to create your rock and stream gardens, you were in bliss, right?"

"Yes, it was most definitely blissful. I could work all day in those gardens and still want more."

Sonya lit up, "That's what life is *for*—to pursue your passions—even if those desires turn out to be ultimately unsatisfying! It's the anticipation and the process that matters, even more than the end result. When there's passion in the process, that's how magnificent discoveries, symphonies and all sorts of masterpieces come into existence."

She grasped my hand. "And, I see your next passion already forming in you."

"What? I don't understand," I said.

"Aren't you chasing God?"

"Well yes," I admitted, "with not much success."

"You're on this tour, right? God is revealed in the divine expressions of human life—the creations—and even the events you judge as mistakes! I think life should be a treasure hunt for bliss and *Bliss can be another name for God*. Following the trail toward bliss can lead us to life's goal—a goal that changes and reveals itself as we grow.

"So let's go out and look for today's clues. Something or someone will cause a crack to form in your armor. You'll know when it happens. And you'll start to heal."

Tears began to roll down my face again because Sonya herself, with her unconditional loving, had caused a lightening, a feeling of relief. Motherless since I was three years old, this nurturing was like a rain shower on my dry internal landscape. Maybe something could bloom yet.

Sleep came finally and then dawn flashed through that offending window.

Morning sunshine bathed the big plane and caused animated conversations to swell among the passengers as they peered out the windows at the Brazilian landscape coming into view.

I wearily opened my eyes and was struggling to orient myself when a handsome male face swam into view.

Jack, our tour director, bent over Sonya to check on me. "You're Jo, right?"

I mutely nodded my head.

"I was told you were badly hurt and bleeding." He leaned forward and his warm hand squeezed my shoulder.

That woke me up.

The hand moved to my cheek and with a caressing touch he turned my face to where he could see my eyebrow. After a searching look into my eyes, his fingers gently brushed my hair away from the injury and he examined the wound.

I wondered if the rest of my hair was standing on end.

"The cut is in your eyebrow and will soon disappear," he pronounced. With a quick smile and a wink, he turned to leave saying, "I'll see you two ladies when we land."

Sonya grinned at me, a distinct twinkle in her eyes.

I realized that I had been mute during the whole encounter. *He was acting like a responsible tour director, checking out my injury... but that touch on my cheek and that look we exchanged was not standard procedure.*

Man! For so long now, I hadn't thought of myself as a sexual woman. Rusty gears turned in my brain, trying to adjust to this new perspective.

After quickly surveying myself in the plane's cramped washroom mirror, I decided that although "of a certain age", my generously curved body was still pretty well preserved thanks to all that heavy gardening, and my auburn hair, now flecked with silver, looked pretty good.

"Okay, Jo McRae," I told the mirror, "It's high time you learned how to play again. But I bet old Jack is a card-carrying *professional* player with his pick of several younger women on this tour. Trolling the waters, he's dangling that sexy bait of his to see who bites. Get a Grip! Don't be played for a silly middle-aged fool!"

TAOISM *"By doing to others as you would wish to be done by, and being sincere and honest in all your dealings, you may attract all men to become your friends."*

The Su Shu, Part III

---

2 Jack

Jack paced back and forth in his cramped hotel room, talking to himself. It was almost time to meet his new tour group at the airport. *What possessed me to advertise my tour in a <u>religious</u> magazine? Probably got a bunch of serious, judgmental seniors, and have to work my ass off to pump any life into the trip.*

Even though his television show aired on the History Channel, he wondered why *religious* people would sign up for a tour with his talks of out-of-body experiences, near-death experiences, evidence of extra-terrestrial visitations and unfamiliar religions such as that of the Mayans.

"Well," he muttered, "My ad *was* in 'Whole Spirit' and it *does* feature articles from *all* the major religions. Rigid fundamentalists wouldn't dare look into other faiths; lightening might strike 'em! " He grinned to himself.

Part of his motivation to attract an older population came as a result of his last tour. That rowdy bunch of young people had run him ragged trying to stay ahead of them and he had mistakenly romanced the most energetic woman of the trip. Keeping up with her, he had almost popped a hernia!

Pulling on light-weight pants for the tropics, he grunted approval of the mirror's exposé and noticed the loose waist band. The little folds of middle age hanging over his belt loops were gone. Those gut-wrenching trips to the gym had paid off.

One of the "perks" of leading tours was that some of the women would potentially have the fantasy of an exotic liaison in mind. It was exhilarating to be admired by them as an expert. And tour romances left no expectations of commitment—just his cup of tea. But this time he'd pick a woman with some age on her, instead of a creatively daring and insatiable young woman.

But, *absolutely no double-dipping!* It had become his primary tour rule after succumbing to the lovely temptations of *two* women on a past trip. There was screaming and hair-pulling before *that* fiasco of a tour was over.

He bent to the bed to sort through his equipment, and counted off the well-worn list in his head. The last thing he always did was call his mother to tell her goodbye, but no more. Alzheimer's disease had taken away too much of her mind and he was grateful for his sister who cared for her through this long battle.

A hollow ache spread across his chest as he missed talking to the one woman who had loved him regardless of his transgressions (and self-centered life). That hollow feeling would have been labeled by his "ex" as an empty chest cavity—no heart.

Shaking it off, he grabbed the laptop to see if any new developments were listed on the extraterrestrial web site he frequented.

"Bingo!" A new sighting in Peru had happened two days before, witnessed by a whole church congregation. Those people swore that a perfect circle of lights appeared in the sky as they left the evening service, and then burst apart and shot off at incredible speeds. One of his presentations was filmed right near that spot. "Alright!"

The airport had provided a space to collect and greet his new tour group. What an odd assortment of people, all ages and cultures, by the look of them. It would have been difficult to assemble a more eclectic bunch. Several attractive women caught his eye and his spirits raised a notch. No one seemed stiff and pompous—the religious personality he had feared.

Boarding the plane had gone well and he sank thankfully into his seat for the long trip.

The Flight

Shit! I'm such an idiot! How can a veteran flyer like myself hurl my supper all over these new slacks?

When he woke a few minutes ago, the plane had turned into an amusement park ride, first dropping straight down and then flinging the fear-ridden passengers left and right.

His dinner had reappeared in its altered state. Luckily, as always on tours, he had positioned himself in the back of the plane so enthusiastic members wouldn't keep him awake all night. The unfortunate man next to him took one look at the nasty display on his seatmate's pants and barfed too. They looked helplessly at each other because their plane was still pitching and dropping dangerously.

Finally, after it steadied, neither of them waiting for the seatbelt sign to be turned off, they both bolted for one of the four bathrooms in the back to scrape away the evidence. Soapy paper towels helped a lot and Jack hoped the dark brown slacks would be somewhat presentable after they dried.

Returning to his seat, he noticed a lot of commotion in the front where his group was sitting. A flight attendant raced by and he asked what had happened.

"A woman's head is bleeding from an impact with the window-frame," she said.

He stood up and strained to see. *It looked like that pretty redhead!* Since he couldn't stand the sight of blood, and they seemed to have it covered, he decided, *I'll check on her when my pants are dry.*

When it was morning, he worked his way through the plane to the woman (he'd looked up her name) and said, "You're Jo, right?"

When she nodded he said, "The flight attendant told me you were hurt?"

She nodded again and pointed to her forehead. A small Band-Aid over the blue swollen lump, and no blood, thank God. She looked back at him with hazel eyes and he felt a little tug; nicely ripe for the picking, even with tired eyes and lumpy brow.

Rio

Upon entering the Rio de Janeiro airport he mischievously thought, *Rio! One of my favorite cities.* Tour groups always reacted strongly to first contact with all that bare skin on the beach, and he relished their shock.

After the scheduled "settling into the hotel period," he charged down to the lobby to talk to the bus driver. No bus. No driver.

Aggravated, he turned to his dependable iPhone which produced the needed phone numbers and solutions. "It's on the way" in South

America can mean anything—but ten minutes later the big blue bus groaned to a stop at their curb.

Herding and head counting began. He would count heads all day. Three silver-haired ladies would be last each time, always needing an extra bathroom trip. He courteously smiled and patted their arms with concern when they finally appeared.

Happily, no more unexpected screw-ups challenged the rest of the day.

That night, after watching those three elderly ladies fluster around at the near-nudity on each beach, he positioned himself where he could observe them as they encountered the Mulata show. Once, he laughed out loud, when a male high-kicking, karate-chopping dancer practically thrust his crotch up their noses, at their front, corner table. *That would give them something to talk about back home!*

After everyone was reseated on the bus, he noticed the show must have gotten Mildred, one of the little old ladies, slightly over-heated because she crowded up to Jo's face and started ranting about sin, the devil and repentance. *Why Jo?* But the redhead held her composure and weathered the storm—very admirable on her part.

She seemed to have attached herself to the little Indian woman Sonya, and the Muslim woman. It would be tougher to "cut her out of the pack" and make his move. As an after-thought he wondered how the Muslim woman was coping with the open-minded flagrant sexuality that oozed out of Rio.

Next day's brunch was very successful, thankfully. His restaurant of choice had been highly recommended, but he was nervous until the food proved to be good and the musical trio outstanding.

"Out of Body Experiences"

That night, as he stepped up to the podium for his "Out of Body" talk, the room was filled to capacity. The hotel had agreed to put his poster in the lobby and other guests came, filling the seats. Some pretty young women were holding his book and waving it, so the book signing afterward might prove interesting. He began...

"My subject tonight is Out of Body Experiences. Starting when I was an adolescent, I experienced these out-of-body episodes and they continue to this day. The early ones were spontaneous, and I couldn't control the timing or where I "went". It was scary—I didn't know enough, at the time.

"I would lie in bed at night and it seemed like a huge, vibrating energy would take over my body. When I got too scared, it would stop. But the experiences were so exciting; I overcame my fear with curiosity and finally "got out". I would fly over the city and visit different places.

"Eventually, as I got better and braver," he flashed a smile, "I went out of this world to bizarre realms and probably different dimensions.

"After mentioning these episodes, I got negative reactions from my parents, pastor and from the counselor I was sent to see for these 'delusions'. So, I shut up about it and wrestled with the suspicion that I might be going crazy. Continuing to explore the 'trips', I slowly began to learn ways to control the fear of not being able to get back *in* my body."

He glanced out at his audience and was gratified to observe enthralled and fearful expressions on most of the faces (especially the young women). One of the silver-haired ladies raised a tentative arm, signaling a question.

Jack said, "Yes?"

In a shaking voice she asked, "How did you decide you *weren't* crazy?"

Gleeful laughter erupted from everyone and she tried to explain, "I mean, back then, how did you…?"

Jack gallantly rescued her by stepping down to stand by her chair and with his hand on her shoulder said, "I'm not one hundred percent sure about my sanity *today!*"

Amid happy laughter he resumed the podium.

"As the years went by, more information became available. The practice of deep meditation seemed to bring my mind to the right state to promote the experience and I learned to initiate episodes.

"It was very important," he said, "to ask for an experience that would be for my highest good and protected by God. Before learning that, I had some frightening trips into several violent 'realms' out there."

After telling about his own experiences, Jack described other unique episodes that people had shared with him at the conclusion of his lectures. He impressed the audience with the idea that there were unlimited dimensions or realms to be explored.

Amid the generalized clamor to get to him at the end of the talk, he strategically herded everyone toward his book table and display, to hopefully make some money. Several pretty girls did buy his book and then lingered to chat.

The tall willowy blond, Rita, in his tour group, stayed the longest and made it quite obvious that she was interested in some extra-curricular activity. Although she was enticing, he didn't like the fact that she was so easy, so available. Scanning the tour members, his eyes fell on a familiar redhead. Something about Jo intrigued him and he decided to patiently pursue the source of that magnetic draw.

MUSLIM *"We believe in Allah and that which is revealed to us, and that which was revealed to Abraham and Ishmael and Isaac and Jacob and the tribes, and that which was given to Moses and Jesus and to the prophets from their Lord; we make no distinction between any of them, and to Him we submit."*

Qur'an 3:84

---

3 Rio

The Brazilian runway rushed up to greet us and the touch-down of our giant plane was so smooth as to be almost imperceptible. *How can they do that?* I wondered.

As we filtered through the airport and claimed our bags, the tour group members seemed to gradually segregate themselves into religious categories. Jews gravitated to Jews, Christians to Christians and so forth. It seems to be human nature to congregate with like-minded people; however, my agenda was different. I *wanted* variety.

The friendship with Sonya was a good start, but I yearned to get to know more of the tour members. It seemed awkward to just charge over to a clump of people and insert myself, so I decided to hold back and wait for some sort of opening.

Humid, warm tropical air enveloped us as we exited the airport and stood on the sidewalk amid the crowd. Overdressed, we envied the cool, somewhat transparent clothing of the people around us— we envied their comfort with bare brown shoulders, arms and legs warmed by the sun. Even the hefty mamas escorting their children sauntered with a conscious pride in their bodies while they chattered in the Portuguese language.

As if to enhance the culture shock, a tour of two famous beaches was first on the agenda. Our group stood on a wide black and white tiled walkway that separated the street from Copacabana Beach. This beach seemed to attract families and older people.   Ipanema Beach was next with yet a different patterned black and white tile walkway bracketed by abundant, wind-whipped palm trees. A strong ocean breeze tossed everyone's hair and clothes into disarray, but given the electrifying view around us, few really noticed the tiles or even the wind.

Beautiful, voluptuous female derrieres were everywhere, not hidden by the skimpy little thong swim suits. The men's swimming attire was also the briefest possible, and I had to say, the view was rather nice.

Before us was a grand display of the "rites of passage" for youth. Serious volley ball games shared the space with large playful sand castles. The inevitable destructions of the sand masterpieces caused laughter, not wars. Frisbees sailed high as energetic young people swirled around us.

They reminded me of my cousins and long-ago days of summer when we skipped through the yard sprinkler with no regard to the clothes we wore. I wondered if in our search for morality, we had mistakenly lost that innocence of youth.

Sonya and I noticed one tour member, an apparent Muslim, judging from her scarf-covered head, long sleeves and skirt, all of which the wind was trying to dismantle. She stood frantically grabbing her billowing clothes, as if she didn't know what to do with her body, and couldn't find a place to hide. When it was time to break for lunch, I grabbed Sonya's arm and we slid into seats at the woman's table.

After introducing ourselves, we found she was Muslim and a Sufi, originally from Pakistan, but had lived in the "States" for twenty years. Her name was Medina. We enthusiastically chatted about the amazing culture of body exposure all around us.

Medina said, "I was taught in Pakistan that our men are basically simple folk and that the mere sight of long gorgeous hair could incite and tempt them into acts of aggressive sexuality. No telling *what* would happen if they were to see these women hanging it all out for Allah and everyone." She giggled, and Sonya and I laughed out loud.

Medina went on in a joking manner and guessed that we felt sorry for Muslim women having to wear such restricting and hot clothing. "You have it all wrong. I can go out shopping without having to comb my hair or shave my legs!"

Again there was a general laughing around the table.

Medina was a young, attractive woman; her scarf and clothing had a beautiful flowing style and color, somewhat like Sonya's sari. The hair that framed her face had a habit of refusing to stay covered completely and its black luster matched her beautiful dark eyes.

Lunch finished, the three of us took in the sights together. Rio sprawls along the gently curving shore of Guanabara Bay and the setting was quite stunning with Sugar Loaf Mountain, at one end, like a punctuation mark! We went on the tour of Sugar Loaf with its cable car that has been around since 1912 (hopefully, refurbished from time to time). The view of Rio from the top was breathtaking, and we could even see our next destination, the gigantic Christ the Redeemer statue sitting on top of the opposite mountain, Corcovado.

That night we *really* got to experience Rio and its unique culture. Historically, slave trade was prevalent in Brazil so the black population is large, about one third, unlike the other South American countries.

"Plataforma" is a show that displays the blending of African and Brazilian music, dance and folklore. That night, thirty beautiful Mulata women dancers and the male cast took us on a cultural journey of African percussion, Capoeira (martial arts/dance) and *samba!* Again, not much skin was covered up. The finale was a parade of elaborate carnival costumes. Once again, I was struck with how sexuality is absolutely celebrated in Rio.

As we were walking out to the bus I noticed that Mildred, one of the silver-haired ladies, was very agitated. The other two looked embarrassed and confused.

"Lucifer is here! The fallen angel of the Lord, *Satan* is loose in Rio—and in that club! Those men were shaking their *genitals* in our faces!"

She zeroed in on me, in the seat across the aisle and shook her little crucifix. "Do you have a personal relationship with Jesus Christ?"

Now *I* was confused!

She popped back up out of her seat and got in my face. "I saw how you enjoyed that black man when he danced for you—so close—his sweat probably splattered on your chest! Sin! Sin! Sin!

"You *have* to have a personal relationship with Jesus to *save* you when you are tempted. We have it!" She gestured at her companions but then turned back to me and said, "You are younger and vulnerable. Lucifer is breathing down your neck!" Abruptly, she seemed to come to her senses and sat back down in silence.

I was humiliated. It didn't matter that she was the one out of control. It didn't matter that I *wasn't* young. She was right. I was aroused by the undulations of the dance, the close interaction of male/female dancers. Illogically, I felt *guilty.*

And she had done the one thing that had historically turned me *off* Jesus. She was in my face with *the* question, "Do you have a personal relationship with Jesus Christ?" *What was that?*

After successfully controlling my flood of emotions on the bus, I hurried to my room and almost whacked Sonya with the door as I slammed it. Sonya and Medina slid inside and said nothing for several minutes. They waited, almost as if in anticipation of the coming tirade.

"That's what ruins Christianity for me! Judgment!" I raved and paced around my bed. "It's so black and white to them."

Medina hesitantly said, "I think you were the target of a loving but misguided attempt to *save* you. Moses brought the Ten Commandments down off his mountain to save his primitive, child-like, volatile people who *needed* some directions. Untamed aggressions, closely tied to sexuality, have destroyed many cultures throughout history. The Jews brought order to their people, and strong rules to live by.

"You Christians and we Muslims inherited those Jewish guidelines and benefited from them. In my country of Pakistan, women's bodies are covered to minimize the temptations of sexuality. Our cultural consciousness of the past required it."

Sonya added, "As we mature in our spiritual and cultural awareness, some of those safeguards become unnecessary. We self-govern and our understandings grow. We begin to judge *their* ways as backwards, wrong. But they are necessary until their group consciousness changes."

I plopped down and stretched out on my bed, calmed by her words. Jesus did come to give us the next step. He said that all those

Jewish laws were secondary to the first two commandments: *Love your God with all your heart, and love your neighbor as yourself.* That takes care of all the rest. Heaped under guilt and shame, because all those rules were so often broken, people *did* need Jesus' love and forgiveness.

Offering reassurance, Medina said, "Mildred, your little old lady, was trying to give you that love in her own way. She was obviously stirred up by all that rampant sexuality and was sounding the alarm. *"Satan is in the house. Emergency measures are called for! Repent!"*

I laughed until tears fell on my smile. Heavy judgment was erased by the gentle salve of forgiveness.

Medina pulled me up off the bed and hugged me. "We're all alike you know. We're just wonderful, lumpy, prickly, unique versions of humanity."

I looked at her in wonderment. *A Muslim who honored the Jewish prophet Jesus, explaining His love, to heal me, a "back-sliding" Christian.*

Brazilian Jazz

Since it was a long and eventful evening, everyone was rewarded with a chance to "sleep in". This was followed, the next morning, by a tasty brunch featuring distinctive Brazilian progressive Jazz— presented by a trio of flute, bass, and guitar.

The musicians who bent over their instruments weren't young. They were in fact, aged, tenderized by time, like the excellent prime rib roast we were eating. That fact gave an added depth to their music—a knowing, an understanding that *only having lived through it could afford.*

I gazed at the wrinkled woman bent over her flute and a roller coaster of emotions sprang from my chest as she seemed to play my "life review", explored through sound-evoked emotion, not content. Busy, productive youth, told in breathy, staccato sounds. Grief, "dark nights of the soul", spoken in mournful, wailing, despairing notes, never to rise again. But "Yes!" delicious, sensual pleasure erupted from her flute as syncopated Brazilian Jazz. She silently encouraged the bass to organize and steady her with its grounding beat; cooperating, alternating with the playful, joyous guitar held by a skinny, bent man who fairly danced with his instrument. It was a *remembrance,* a dance of life in sound.

How could musical notes bypass the brain and communicate with us all on such a deep level?

I couldn't sing or play a note on any instrument, but I could understand and relate to that universal, musical language. It gave a whole new meaning to the term "soul music."

I noticed Jack off to one side, with a wide grin plastered all over his face. Catching his eye, I smiled and made the "thumbs up" sign.

Shopping

The rest of the afternoon was open. The group could either participate in a bus tour around the town or stroll through plentiful shops within walking distance. Sonya, Medina and I wanted to check out the shops and as we clambered down some stairs, Jack materialized, brushed up against my arm and then paused and smiled. A big neon sign would not have been more noticeable, *available, if you're game.* And I was tempted—was softening— but not yet.

As we three women strolled up and down the streets, we were happy to find fascinating shops to investigate. Exorbitant price tags caused a hurried exodus from a few.

Around the corner from the main shopping area was a tiny store, display windows overflowing with an abundance of beautiful scarves.

Medina squealed with joy and through the door we went. The owner, a Muslim woman from Turkey, had realized the need of Muslim women everywhere to express their personality even within the restrictions placed upon them. She had searched the markets for attractive scarves, and spread out her bounty for us.

Rachael and I bought one each and Medina bought ten! She said, "You have no idea how difficult it is to find beautiful scarves with the right shape and fabric that will stay where you put it. This woman knew what we needed and chose specifically for us."

We grinned at her and she defiantly put her hands on her hips and said, "Well, they don't take up much room in my suitcase!"

She took so long making her choices that I decided to find the restroom. Seated, my eyes fell on a small spouted watering can sitting next to the commode. It was filled with water.

We finally left the shop and I mentioned the little watering pot, having found no plants in the place.

Medina actually blushed as she laughed at me. "The water is for a woman to clean herself. Where bidets are available we don't need them, but she didn't have a bidet. Turkish women always have the little pots." (Another insight to practices in different cultures)

Jack's Agenda

The anticipation was palpable that evening as we poured into the hotel meeting room for Jack's lecture on "Out of Body Experiences." Word must have gotten around because there were strangers filling up the chairs. Finally, everyone settled down and Jack began to speak.

He was good. He handled his subject *and* the audience with enthusiasm and ease. What an intriguing fellow—both knowledgeable and charismatic. He circled around his "hens", even the older ones, with a cocky possessive attitude.

During a generalized clamoring to get to Jack at the end of the talk, I noticed several pretty girls stayed the longest. He seemed to enjoy the strokes to his ego, and was happily signing his books. That tall blonde on our tour, Rita, was practically sitting in his lap as we left.

I stopped by the public restroom on the way out, and was about to come out of a stall when I heard the three silver-haired ladies enter. I cowered down. *Oh no, not Mildred!*

One woman said, "That Jack is a rascal! He's such a flirt!"

The second woman broke in, "But he's so *sweet.* Look how he came down and rescued me after I called him crazy."

Mildred said, "Oh, he's sly all right. Look at you! He's won you over, too. I saw him leaving with that sexy Rita. I bet they're going to *do it* tonight."

"Mildred!" the second woman exclaimed. "It's none of our business!"

Mildred was on a rampage again. She said, "This whole country is of the devil! Sex, sex, sex! That's all they think about here. I'm surprised that a religious tour would include such a place. I feel like I'm looking at Sodom and Gomorrah. We all might turn to pillars of salt!"

The other two howled with laughter and that just made her angrier. "You mark my words—there will be hell to pay!"

They finished and left. I stood, immobile in the stall. *Well, Jo, that's it. No playing with Jack.*

Luxuriating in a temporarily private room, I was grateful my scheduled roommate would arrive for the tour two days late. Then we would trade, as Sonya had asked to be my permanent roommate after tonight.

Jack's out-of-body evidence swirled around in my head and seemed to fit with my own belief systems. After devouring the books by Dolores Cannon, my perspective had widened quite significantly. Dolores, a thirty year veteran hypnotherapist, began practicing traditional hypnotherapy back in the 1960's. Over the years, she specialized in past-life regression and past life therapy. Due to the deep level of trance that her clients were able to reach while under hypnosis, many began to experience past-lives and other levels of existence, dimensions similar to those described by Jack.

One client, a devout fundamentalist Christian, was appalled to be shown a past life where she was a man and a teacher of Jesus in the reclusive Jewish Essene community of Qumran, near where the Dead Sea Scrolls were discovered.

Many of Dolores's clients, no matter their countries or religious orientations, would also talk about life-between-lives. At the close of the deepest sustained regression sessions, a familiar "voice" or "collective entity" came through to answer big picture questions, such as why this client was shown particular past-lives or why he or she was experiencing chronic health issues, poor relationships, or ongoing pain and suffering. Dolores called this wise voice the collective unconscious, given that it appeared to be available to most all who asked while under extremely deep hypnosis.

By delving into Dolores Cannon's paradigm-shaking books, I admit that I had stepped out of my usual comfort zone in my studies of spirituality. However, I acknowledged that along with the advancements man has made with technology and science, there had been parallel advancements in understanding the workings of the human mind.

The new frontier seemed to be internal; exploring the different facets of this glorious thing we call the mind. The five senses have been joined with other levels of perception, and part of this was not new. Bible stories told of prophets receiving visions and instructions from God. Spiritual mystics of all faiths continued through the centuries to meditate deeply in search of God and wrote volumes of information, but it was discounted, suppressed and many people were even persecuted until recently.

Now, I saw a boomerang effect. The interest in paranormal communications like channeling and regressive hypnotherapy, near-death experiences and out-of-body experiences had resurfaced.

We happily sit right in the middle of a flood of information practically pouring down over our heads. Our task is to keep our minds open and consider the new information while using discernment of mind and heart.

After staying up until the wee hours of the night, pondering these mind-opening (or mind-blowing) revelations, the sound of my morning wake-up call came too soon.

Then we were off to Iguazu Falls!

HINDUISM *"I am the same to all beings. I favor none, and I hate none. But those who worship Me devotedly, they live in Me, and I in them. Even the most sinful, if he worship Me with his whole heart, shall be considered righteous, for he is treading the right path. He shall attain spirituality ere long, and Eternal Peace shall be his. O Arjuna! Believe me, My devotee is never lost."*

The Bhagavad Gita, Chapter 9

---

4 Iguazu Falls

Our destination, the spectacular horseshoe-shaped Iguazu Falls, was created by the collision of the Paraná and Iguazu rivers during a volcanic eruption. The falls are taller than Niagara and are four times as wide. Three countries' borders meet at the falls: Argentina, Brazil and Paraguay.

We were delighted with our hotel, a one story, U-shaped building, situated close to the base of the falls. As soon as we moved into our rooms, a helicopter ride was available to get the complete picture from above.

Sonya, Medina and I scurried to the front of the line. Sonya, filled with child-like exuberance, chose the front seat with the pilot and we were off. She rode the dips and turns of the flight like a cowboy on a bucking horse, while we clung to the seat belts and handles in the back.

From this new vantage point, it was immediately obvious that the sheer magnitude of the falls could not be appreciated from below. Goose bumps rose on my arms as I took in the primordial expanse of rain forest which stretched as far as the eye could see. It appeared as a slightly curved horizon of green, slashed by a deep bottomless cleft into which perpetual water was pouring, from all sides. A timeless thing, water had been pouring just like this for eons.

With humbleness, I realized again, what little specks we are on this magnificent Earth. Once before, in New Mexico, I had experienced this *awe* as I looked up at the Milky Way and saw it for the first time, without the veil of civilization's ever-present lights and humidity. The southwest skies revealed a seemingly infinite miracle of space. Inhaling the profound beauty, my mind and heart nearly burst.

I was reminded of the joke about a frog that lived in an old well. One day an ocean frog came to visit and as they swam around in the well, the well frog bragged about the mossy rocks and the great depth and vastness of his home. With a twinkle in his eye, the ocean frog invited his host to come to visit the sea. When they arrived at the seashore, the well frog took one long look at the expanse of ocean, and his head exploded! I felt a little like that well frog as I tried to take in the enormity of Iguazu Falls.

Back to earth, as the helicopter landed, heat and humidity enveloped us. We searched for the stairs to the falls which were nearly invisible because of the invading jungle foliage. Finding them, we clambered down wet, mossy stone steps to the bottom, grateful for a lone handrail.

And Oh, the Falls! The sound and the roar of all that water crashing past us to the river below made speech impossible. Struck dumb, we tried to take in the thundering, heavy power while mist coated our hair, eyelashes and clothes. To experience it with friends, to share it, only amplified the joy.

At last, we returned to the steamy steps and began to climb up and up, and up. The jungle around us seemed to move and tremble! Hidden in the deep foliage was an entire colony of Lemurs! First one, then two, then a whole family of the little long-legged, raccoon-striped animals followed us up the path while staying just out of reach. They didn't seem to want food, perhaps only curious? It felt like a sort of reverse zoo—the animals watched and were entertained *by us.*

Ending our day's adventure, we three women spilled into the lobby of the hotel—damp, hot, wrinkled and worn out. There, we were presented with a tray containing a national pleasure, a *Pisco* Sour. Each little glass was cold and inviting to the fingers and the combination of lovely lime juice, sugar and the local brandy slid down our throats like heaven. Medina, with her practice of no alcohol, asked for one with no brandy, just lovely lime juice and sugar.

The *Pisco* Sour, exhilaration, fatigue, heat and exhaustion resulted in a divine comedy of sorts, as we three roommates went to take a shower.

A hitch in the accommodations had caused the three of us to need to share a room. Ours must have been the honeymoon suite. The shower was clear glass, and visible from the main room, with no door to shut. I was sticky and *stinky* so, taking the situation in stride and summoning up my courage, I stepped into the extremely visible enclosure first, embarrassed and determined. The other two shielded their eyes and pretended not to look.

Stunned, I realized the water was ice cold! No amount of working the faucets affected it at all. So, quickly soaping and rinsing, I pretended it was wonderful, grabbed my towel and exited, invitingly spreading an arm into a "your turn" motion. Sonya was next, and she gasped, shuddered, got the joke, braced herself, and did the same, covering it well. She grinned wide, having finished, and made the invitation to Medina.

With the first blast of cold water, Medina screamed! Then she laughed almost hysterically, totally naked and dancing with cold, our Muslim buddy. We giggled and wiggled, snorted and cavorted, inadequately covering our frigid curves with soggy little towels.

Bonding as women was absolutely complete. It was impossible to retain *any* barriers while naked.

Medina

Afternoon in the tropics encourages relaxation and rest. We lay back on the beds but sleep was illusive. Sonya asked, "How did you come to be on this trip, Medina?"

A strange expression passed across Medina's face as she tried to decide whether to be frank with us. Satisfied that we could be trusted with her secrets, she began her story.

"I grew up in Pakistan twenty years ago. Today, most of the country is westernized in dress and culture, very modern, although the women still cover their hair and bodies to be modest. But twenty years ago it was a firmly controlled patriarchal culture. Most women didn't become educated, only men.

"My father was originally a Hindu from India and of the *Rajput,* the highest Indian caste. He converted to Islam years ago and *walked* the whole distance to the new Muslim country, Pakistan. He raised and educated me with the privileges of a male even though it wasn't the accepted practice. I didn't have to do women's work and he taught me to drive him around in his car, *an unheard of privilege for a woman.*" As she warmed to her story, she sat up on the side of her bed and straightened her shoulders. "He said I was smarter than my brothers."

"All wealthy Pakistani men go away to college, university, in the United States or England, and I expected to do the same. But when I was twenty years old, he announced that I should marry. I fought him. I wanted only an education, not marriage. He explained that he would find a suitable match, with my approval—one of our caste, who was going to the United States to school—one who would *promise* to provide my education within the marriage."

"Since I wanted an education above all else, and romance was second, I realized my father had better resources for finding that opportunity. So, we agreed on a husband, from the choices he found. I saw pictures of my potential mate. I really wanted to meet him but I could not, as he was in England. So, I made the practical decision, to marry. In the end, I had to trust the process."

Sonya interrupted, "How did you know that your husband would keep his promise, to provide for your education?"

Medina looked at us, incredulous at the idea. "He is of the *Rajput* caste also, and honorable. He would never break his word."

We looked at her and each other in amazement. To marry without any idea of the "chemistry", the sexual attraction between the male and female, was so foreign to us.

I remarked, "Come to think of it, just relying on physical attraction sure hasn't resulted in a whole lot of long-term, successful marriages, either."

Sonya said, "My Hindu father tried to arrange a marriage for me, but I refused. It caused a terrible rift in our relationship. Eventually, I chose the love of my life."

"So we married," Medina continued. "We went to Salt Lake City, Utah, for his doctorate in Medicine. I managed to birth and care for two children, while finishing my undergraduate economics degree, *as valedictorian of that huge class.*" The pride was evident in her eyes.

I broke in and asked, "So how is it in the bedroom?"

Medina looked at me, amazed that I would ask so intimate a question. I blushed, but waited for an answer.

She replied truthfully. "It is quite good, actually. Mutual admiration, purpose, and consideration can form a bond that transcends the primal attraction of male and female. Most marriages that survive the decline of the initial passionate beginning arrive at the trusting, loving, and considerate level. That is where we started, although, I must admit, the passion and attraction <u>did</u> develop. When I decided to trust the process, I surrendered, and everything came together.

"When it was time for my husband to choose a city to work in, he was considerate of my wishes and we agreed on Little Rock, Arkansas because I could go to the Clinton Presidential school to complete my Masters, in Public Service.

"I now work free-lance in economic development, with projects in communities all over the world that are trying to overcome poverty and other problems."

"But I have two *passions,*" she said. "First, I really want to help the women of Pakistan in the border towns near Afghanistan. There, they are still poorly treated, like possessions, slaves, *animals.* This summer, while my children visited their grandparents and cousins in a safe part of Pakistan, I went to work in a dangerous border town. I had a leadership role and the men on the project resented receiving directions from a woman.

"It was a bad experience there." She shrugged her shoulders and admitted, "Because of my upbringing, I can't stand stupid men who want to control and dominate me." She stood up and strolled around the room. Even in her robe she had a regal, ruling class presence about her—a sureness of character.

"But I went too far by making the mistake of confronting one obstinate young man when we were alone. I out-ranked him, and challenged him with my eyes when he refused to do his job.

"He flew into a rage, out of control, and knocked my head into the door of a storage area. Stunned, I wasn't quick enough and he pulled me into that tiny room and slammed the door. When I screamed, he toppled a heavy rolled-up carpet over my face and upper body to shut me up.

"I couldn't get a full breath of air and the dust from that rug strangled me. I was suffocating! My mind screamed my rosary prayers. *Glory be to Allah. Praise be to Allah. Allah is the greatest!* At that moment a strong impulse came to kick out—to kick the door and make a lot of noise with my hard shoes. So I kicked out with my legs as he forced them apart for the ultimate degrading act. Frantically, I managed to bang one shoe on the door, and the loud noise brought help. Allah be praised."

I gasped and exclaimed, "Oh, my God!"

"Yes," Medina said, "Oh My God!"

Sonya jumped up and took Medina's hand in her own and squeezed it with sympathy. Medina raised Sonya's hand in hers and kissed it. "Thank you." She bowed her head and continued. "I was rescued and he was eventually punished. She looked up at us and admitted, "Since then, I have a kind of claustrophobia and can't stand to have anything covering my face. I guess my pride caused me to go too far and risk too much.

"My husband and our children fear for my life, and he has forbidden any mention of another of those trips. I guess I'll back off, for a while anyway. He urged me to go on this tour, even arranged for a woman to take care of our children." She smiled as her eyes filled with unshed tears of repressed emotion.

"That first passion, to help Pakistani women is overshadowed by my second, strongest passion. I am training with a Sufi Master *to deeply experience God, to be consumed with God.* I want that experience *now,* and I am frustrated because *that* path doesn't have a controllable time schedule. I constantly do what my Master says; I pray with my prayer beads, and carefully do my Sufi *Qualbi dhikr* meditation—Heart in Remembrance. But I can't *make* that deep experience of God happen like I can control other things in my life.

"So I am here on this trip representing my faith, trying to promote understanding and good will; trying to make others understand that the Muslim terrorists seen on the news do not represent Islam. And, I'm taking a break to get a renewed perspective on my life... my future."

Sonya and I got up and hugged our beautiful Sufi friend. Sonya said, "We are honored that you would share your private thoughts with us. We will keep them safe."

"Medina," I interjected, "You mentioned your prayer beads. I didn't know Muslims had rosaries like our Catholics."

She smiled and said, "I think several religions use them to keep track of their repetitive prayer meditations."

Realizing that it had gotten late, we had to scramble to dress for the evening. As I quickly slipped into my clothes and found my shoes, I thought, *I had no idea Muslims emphasized meditation and intense practices like Medina described. I want to know more about Sufis. Maybe that'll be the key to experiencing God, the feeling I long for.*

HINDUISM *"All the universe has the (Supreme) Deity for its life. That Deity is Truth. He is the Universal Soul."*

The Upanishads

---

5 Near-Death Experiences

Over dinner, Jack spoke of Near-Death Experiences. This time, he had no personal knowledge to share, but had extensive research and stories to tell.

We listened with growing awe, as he shared story after story of people from all over the world. Each had a common thread. Many of these people went to a place of *unconditional love*, and didn't want to come back... at first. Close to death, they were joined by a loving presence and they realized what little importance they now placed on their human lives and bodies. There were beautiful realms to be experienced, deceased acquaintances to greet, and sometimes "Halls of Knowledge" were shown to them by learned spirits. The lucky ones were shown the purpose, the great value of this Earth experience.

Many saw a life review and with each scene, they could feel the emotions of *all* the participants. If they treated someone kindly, they felt the gratitude of that person. Conversely, if they had treated someone unfairly or cruelly, they felt the pain that they had inflicted. The presence watching with them was not a judge, but a loving companion who guided them to greater understanding of how they had done in their living of this existence.

This benevolent spirit seemed to love and value them, regardless of the success or failure of the life they were watching. Sometimes they were so disappointed in themselves that they begged to come back and "get it right." The only judgment it seemed, was *their own.*

With any significant time spent on the other side, the result seemed to unanimously be that these persons were changed forever. Their former priorities shifted. Money and power became unimportant. Accumulating "stuff" and searching for entertainment and pleasure was not a priority. People and relationships and creation in general, became of utmost importance.

Secure in the knowledge they had absorbed on the "other side", their self-worth soared. *They knew that they were valuable, totally loved and needed in the whole scheme of God's plan. Fear, the reigning heavy weight of this earth, dissipated. Joy, purpose and peace became their life.*

Jack looked out at his audience, "I know a lot about out-of-body experiences – OBEs." He shrugged his shoulders and admitted, "But they aren't the same as near-death experiences—NDEs. OBEs don't seem to be as life changing except for the fact that they allow a broader picture of creation—things unexperienced by the five senses."

Jack concluded his talk with the statement, "These near-death experiences *are life changing events!*"

I was so jealous! I wanted some of <u>that</u>!

So, it seemed, did two people sitting next to us. A voluptuous, full-figured woman of middle age, named Rachael and a tall well-built blond young man named Todd. We all pressed into a conversation circle, asking questions and making observations. It became clear we were not done for the evening. So, we adjourned to the coffee shop. Thirty minutes later, with lively banter still flowing, we three roommates had a swift consultation and invited the two new friends to our room. And then we were five.

Clustering on the double beds and in two chairs, discussion began.

"Why is your bathroom shower visible in the bedroom?" asked Rachael.

"We don't know," I answered.

"Isn't it a little awkward?"

Of course we three roommates howled with laughter but couldn't adequately describe the earlier shower experience.

Addressing the two new, very confused people, Sonya lifted her shoulders in a suggestive way and said, "We have become intimate friends."

That closed the topic.

Sonya's Near Death Experience

After we thoroughly rehashed all the info from Jack's latest lecture, Sonya spoke up and said, "I had a near-death experience when I was a young woman."

We begged her to tell us every detail.

She sat up straighter in the chair and smoothed the skirt of her sari across her knees. "My whole life I was a fearful, nervous wreck," she explained. "I was afraid of everything—of cancer, of embarrassing or disappointing my family, of creating bad karma. When it came time for marriage, my father arranged one for me and I refused the man. My father never got over the fact that I disobeyed him and ultimately chose for myself to marry the love of my life. The whole episode scared me that I might have created bad karma! You live a bad life—you get punished in this life or the next.

"Lymphoma developed in my body and after fighting it for four years, it was killing me. When I lapsed into a coma and wouldn't wake up, my husband took me to the hospital.

"Amazingly, I was aware of everything. Still in a comatose state in my room, I was able to see the doctor down the long hall from my room as he told my family that I had less than 36 hours to live.

With tumors everywhere, my organs had nearly shut down. Swollen body and brain, I was dying.

"I heard all this, but couldn't understand it because I was also in a place that felt so *good* and so *light* and so *incredible*, with the *most astounding, embracing unconditional love!*"

She looked at us, throwing out her arms in frustration, "*Love is an inadequate word for what I was feeling. There's really nothing on earth quite like it!*

"I could see all the events of my life but they didn't *seem* to be in the past. It felt like the present and though everything was happening simultaneously, I could still focus on individual events.

"Again, I was in both worlds. I saw the medical caregivers and my family and I could feel their emotions. *I was them. There was no sense of the terribly important, singular ego consciousness, no 'skin' boundary. Without the body that I had left, I saw that we are all one consciousness, all facets of God! The body in this life is a barrier because when we are in it, we lose the ability to feel others' emotions, to be a part of the All.* Because I was in this altered-state, I could see the reality of life on Earth."

Unable to contain himself, Todd exclaimed, "Everyone talks about the 'oneness concept'—that we are all one—you got to *feel* that! For me, it's so much more believable after hearing your experience."

"Yes!" Sonya said, "For whatever reason when in a body, we believe we are separate from the All and have to make it on our own.

So, *fear takes over.* I firmly believe that my lifetime of fear caused my cancer!

"With one foot still in the hospital and the other in the spirit realm, I looked to the right and saw my deceased father. He, who had been so judgmental of my choices because of his religious beliefs, *was total unconditional Love. There was no culture, no time, no religion, only peace and Love.* I decided, if this was dying, so be it. I saw that religion should not promote fear or discord of any kind. That is a *human* mistake.

"My father told me that I couldn't go any further or I would not be able to come back. As I turned my attention to that choice, to go ahead and die, I saw it happening. I saw the doctor telling my family I was dead. I now understood that my husband had chosen to come with me in this life because we had a shared purpose to fulfill. We had planned to create a spiritual community that was open to all who needed it. But I saw that he would die soon after I left, because our purpose had *not* been fulfilled and he couldn't do it alone.

"So, I looked at staying in that body. The pain and deteriorated state of it were so bad that I just didn't want to return to it again." Sonya cringed and shivered at the remembered sight of her grotesque, bloated form lying on the bed.

"But then it was revealed to me that without *fear,* my body would start to heal immediately—much quicker than a normal healing.

"So… I came back. Miraculously, most of the tumors were healed within the first four days! The word got out and doctors came from other countries to study my chart. One amazed doctor said, that I should be dead!" She giggled at the words. Then she sobered up and debated on how to explain what happened next.

"My near death experience took a while to explore and understand," she said. "I knew I had connected with a profound 'Source', but was it God? What was it? My former God was an external, judgmental Being. I *finally* understood that God has no form, no limitations. I had connected with that 'Something' and I became One with It and all that is!"

Sonya stood, as if to help make her next point. She stretched her petite body up, arms wide above her head, fingers apart. "This is <u>important</u> friends. I was shown that when I became 'centered' in the universe, I allowed all that was mine to come to me with no *need* to pursue it. It's not like we thought, that we have to strive to get what we want because there's not enough for all. There is no need for competing because each of us is unique and... what is ours... comes to us.

"We are magnificent Beings! We come from pure Love—at the center we *are* pure Love—and we will return to pure Love!

"Before he returned to that Love, my husband and I stayed with our purpose and accomplished it together, as we were meant to do."

We sat there in silence and looked at each other—each with a personal concept of God—and saw the shared consternation, the mental straining to fit this new puzzle piece into our individual understanding of the Divine.

Medina recited a quote from her precious Sufi poet, Rumi.

"Only from the heart can we reach the sky."

Here we were—Rachael was Jewish, Medina was Muslim, and I, Christian. All came from the same source, Abraham. And then there was Sonya, a Hindu, and Todd who embraced Buddhism and the Tao. We were sitting together and beginning to feel there might really be a common denominator. My urge to find it was strong.

I had one last thought. *To contemplate Sonya's view of God as this formless, limitless, source of Pure Love was quite mind-opening but a little intangible and unfamiliar to me. What about the Presence I have occasionally sensed while writing in my journal or during meditation and prayer? This familiar Presence was more* personal *in nature. Can such a vast, expansive definition of God fit with this personal relationship I had cherished? The common thread running through both viewpoints is Love. What is more personal than that? I felt a sense of peace as I allowed this thought to settle in.*

Departure

The next morning we had our bags outside our doors for pick-up at six a.m. to be loaded for departure to Buenos Aires, Argentina. We then boarded the bus and the bags were stuffed underneath in the storage bins. Only one medium-sized bag was allowed per person, but even so, it was a lot of luggage.

At the airport, we stepped from the bus to find the plane was late. Porters piled our luggage onto four large carts to wait.

I was standing outside watching the same porters seated on milk crates, playing checkers with soda bottle caps on a board drawn with magic markers, when the sound of a woman "wailing" drifted out of the airport door.

Curious, I walked back to see one of the silver-haired ladies weeping and wringing her hands. Jack stood in front of her bent forward, trying to make sense of the melt-down.

She had left her heart medication in the hotel bathroom and had even forgotten to take her morning pill.

After hiding a brief look of aggravation, Jack quickly whipped out his iPhone like a gun from a holster, and called for a taxi to go straight to the hotel. Next, he called the hotel and asked them to retrieve the pill bottle and give the medication to the taxi driver who would be instructed to race it back to us at the airport.

He then spun around to check the runway for the plane. "Darn!" It was rolling up to the airport. "Why can't it be <u>really</u> late when I need it to be?" He muttered.

We all boarded and the luggage was loaded efficiently. The pilot, already behind schedule, was aggravated to be asked for five more minutes for a questionable "medical emergency."

Because it was a small airport, I could watch Jack through my airplane window as he stood on the curb looking down the street, his back ramrod straight with anxiety.

The taxi arrived, just as the pilot decided to leave. We yelled that the medicine was here and Jack bounded up into the plane with a big relieved grin on his face, waving the pill bottle.

We all applauded his miracle.

Then he procured a glass of water and *personally* administered the morning dose to our embarrassed little lady. I heard him assure her as he patted her shoulder that it wasn't the first time heart medication had been forgotten.

He asked, "How do you think I knew how to get it back so fast?" We all laughed with relief.

My heart warmed to him. Instead of anger and accusing eyes, he had treated her with gentleness, consideration and incredible efficiency.

SUFI *"One day your heart will take you to your Lover. One day your soul will carry you to the Beloved. Don't get lost in your pain, know that one day your pain will become your cure."*

RUMI (Jalaludin Mohamad)

---

6 Medina and Islam

After the excitement died down and the flight became boring, we five friends traded seats to sit together and continue the discussions. Rachael asked Medina what it meant to be a Sufi, as she knew very little of it. Everyone chimed in with the request for further explanation.

"First, I am a Muslim; that is Islam", explained Medina.

"The word Islam translates to 'the peace that comes when one's life is surrendered to God.' Our prophet Muhammad was an illiterate orphan descended from the line of Abraham. His Arab world was corrupt, lawless and degenerate. The existing polytheistic religion did nothing to change that fact.

"Muhammad fell in love with a woman who was fifteen years older than himself and he was faithful to her until she died. She owned a caravan and through their travels, the evil world he encountered disturbed his mind. At home, he spent long periods of time—many whole nights—meditating in a cave. One of the gods of the polytheistic religion was Allah, a creator, provider and determiner of destiny. Allah became real to him during his meditations and he saw that 'there is no god but God'— Allah. Other people in Mecca were also beginning to worship only Allah at the same time.

"When Muhammad was about forty years old, the angel Gabriel came to him in the cave and told him he must proclaim Allah as the *only* God. He wrestled with the idea and resisted the angel. Initially, he was an unwilling prophet but, for the next twenty-three years, although illiterate, Muhammad received the words of Allah, the Koran, in manageable portions. The Koran is a grammatically perfect, beautifully poetic, source of Divine knowledge.

"As Muhammad faithfully exalted Allah, he was systematically persecuted and barely escaped from his home in Mecca with a large following. The city of Medina enlisted him to govern and create peace between its five tribes—three of which were Jewish—which he managed to do for ten years.

"Muhammad believed he was an extension of the knowledge of Jewish and Christian prophets before him, although he was never acknowledged by those religions. He taught the same spirituality as the Jewish prophets like Isaiah—justice, compassion and freedom for all—and he taught of Jesus' love for all people. Amazingly, even in those challenging times, Muhammad was able to bring spirituality into daily life, faith into politics and religion to society.

"But the powerful armies of Mecca repeatedly assaulted him and the city of Medina, until he was forced to war. After five years, the armies of Mecca were eventually defeated and the city was converted to Islam—Allah. Ironically, although Muhammad taught the Koran's message—never to attack first—after his death, his armies went on to conquer and convert many more countries."

Rachael said, "So your name is Medina, like the city?"

Medina smiled and said, "My father loved the name."

The Jewish Rachael, was visibly irritated. Her face flushed with emotion and her hands gripped the arms of her seat until the knuckles turned white. She spat out, "Medina, what you say is probably true for you and some Muslims—that Islam is all about peace—but you have to admit the Arab Muslim countries are notorious for spewing out hate for the 'infidels', for aggression against other religions and their geographic neighbors and even their own Muslim sects that don't believe the 'right' way. They think they can do *anything* in the name of Allah!" She bolted out of her seat and fled to the bathroom to keep from blurting out any more caustic words.

I was alarmed by her hasty departure. There was an extended silence and I decided it was indeed "break time" and got up to move around. Other people were up and down stretching and moving about.

After a cooling off period, we straggled back to our seats. No one said a word. Eventually, each person picked up something to look at or read but I doubted if any one of us comprehended what we were reading. Medina sat quietly staring straight ahead, deep in thought.

Rachael turned the pages of a magazine, slapping them over with an abrupt whack! She was clearly still very agitated.

I thought… *This is the end of our alliance, our friendships. How awful that we can't find a way to co-exist when we don't even have a country or sacred lands to quarrel over. This human insanity is rooted so deeply in us that it boils over without warning when we least expect it.*

But Rachael hadn't moved to another seat. Maybe she hoped there was a way back.

After a long, uneasy silence Medina finally spoke, "A Muslim's ideal is peace. Our standard greeting is translated into 'Peace be upon you.' Please don't confuse the political hostilities of radicals with our religion.

"To westerners, the word 'Jihad' is said in the same breath as Muslim. It conjures up scenes of screaming fanatics being lured into war with promises of instant heaven and virgins if they die for Allah. 'Jihad' literally means *extreme exertion*. It has been adopted by the makers of war as a symbol.

"*Muhammad honored and respected other religions.* He warned as he returned from the inevitable wars, *that the most difficult jihad is the extreme wrestling with one's own soul, the internal battle with evil.*"

Medina gazed at us fondly from under her colorful scarf and tried so desperately to help us understand. "Believers of God generate a great deal of energy. As wonderful and thrilling as such engaged energies may be, we all need to pay close attention to where they are leading us. We should be sure that our actions are harming no one. Misguided ideals lead people to kill one another in the name of their God. A holy war is the same, whether it is Jewish, Christian or Muslim, Catholic or Protestant.

"Christian soldiers of the Crusades, having been promised heaven if they died in war, plunged all of Europe into battle for <u>three centuries</u> in the name of 'The Prince of Peace'. The first battles were over religious access to Jerusalem.

"The same madness was seen in World War II, when Japanese Kamikaze pilots valiantly crashed their planes and bodies into United States strongholds under the religious belief that they would earn a swift path to heaven.

"And then there are always the *opportunists*, the professed 'believers' that use religion to mask aggression for their personal or national profit. *War is very profitable for some people.* History books are packed with the same story. Quotes from your Bible and our Koran can be taken out of context or misquoted to support any private evil agenda in the name of religion. The nightly news screams that Muslims are against Christians and Jews. And so we think it is 'news,' forgetting the past.

"Christianity has been identified in the last few years mainly with the very vocal fundamentalist sects, while the moderates and progressive thinkers seem to be silent. We *also* have a silent majority of moderate Muslims and Sufis, but the money and power and headlines are all about the fundamentalist, deeply conservative sects of Islam."

Medina looked us squarely in the eyes and said, "It's so ironic that it took a trip to South America to bring us into the same space, at last, to share with each other. Westerners are so isolated from the beautiful culture that is Islam. You stay in your insulated churches and lives, to look out occasionally with curiosity at a scarf-covered woman at the grocery store and wonder about her life. But then you tune in to the horrific nightly news to see the 'real' Muslims."

I tensed up, bracing myself for a verbal assault from her—but it never came.

Medina went on, "We are embarrassed and heart-broken with that news. We are people just like you—yes—dressed to modestly cover our bodies, but the same. We go about our lives on our *own* insulated paths, raising our children who go to your schools while our men work in your business world. As good Muslims, every year we are obligated to give 2.5% of our estate to the poor around us.

"We pray five times a day. Our prayers are woven in and out, all through our lives, to remember Allah and to constantly try to live as we were taught—to love—like you. And like you, some of us are better at that than others.

"There are no interactions between the cultures to speak of, and we remain ignorant of each other. We should change that—be brave—find ways to do that."

There was a murmur of agreement. I finally exhaled, not even aware that I had been holding my breath.

Rachael quietly sat in her airplane seat—still with us—but silent.

Sufis

"I am a *Sufi* Muslim." Medina continued. "A person of any sect of Islam can be a Sufi. I felt it was important that you know about Islam first and now I will tell you about *my* faith.

"Sufis are the mystical Muslims. Contemplation of God occupies a significant place in every Muslim's life, but we Sufis are *impatient!* We want to encounter God directly in this very lifetime, *now!*

"We have our masters—our shaikhs who teach us—and we get together to sing, dance and recite our rosaries. This desire for drawing closer to God is practiced in three ways, the mysticisms of *Intuition, Love* and *Ecstasy.*

"Intuitive mysticism brings knowledge. The heart is an organ of <u>discernment</u>. We can see with the 'eye of the heart.' As that sight expands, it begins to see all of God's creations, not as they appear to the world, but as the Spirit within. To the 'eye of the heart,' the world is God-in-disguise."

Grateful that the group seemed to have relaxed into one of our normal conversations, I said, "That is just what we are taught in *A Course in Miracles,* the Christian study infused with Jesus' message. We're to look for the Divine within all people."

Sonya chimed in, "That's what I saw in my near-death experience— the Spirit inside everyone."

Todd said, "In Buddhism, we are asked to *wake up* from this dream world we see. The Sanskrit root word "*budh*" means to wake up and to know."

Quietly and a bit reluctantly, Rachael spoke, "It is written in the Jewish tradition that before we came into the world we *were* all-knowing. At birth an angel came and 'filed away' our insights into our subconscious mind. So the aim of life's journey with its pitfalls, challenges and diversions, is to squeeze the 'grape' that we are, so that the wine—the original all-knowingness—comes out. We are then called to share this 'wine' with the world."

"What you told us is so beautiful," I laughed, "but sometimes that *squeezing* is pretty rough!"

"Yes! So true," the group agreed.

Medina continued with her information. "I told you Intuitive mysticism is seeing with the 'eye of the heart'. The heart also loves. Love mysticism also yields knowledge. We Sufis yearn for the love of God, trying to heal the imagined separation from Him. We yearn for Him and we find that the Beloved, God, yearns for us ***even more!*** That Love spawns a 'knowing'."

"Medina, what about the mysticism of Ecstasy?" I asked. "Love and Ecstasy in the same sentence… sounds intriguing. Didn't Rumi write some very *sensuous* and *intimate* love poetry?" I added playfully.

There seemed to be an invisible leaning forward, a heightened awareness of the group.

Medina smiled and agreed on the sensuousness of Rumi's poetry. "Ecstatic mysticism is best represented by deeply spiritual Sufis who meditate and reach states of bliss and ecstasy. They often have trances and visions—experiences that bring them knowledge and wisdom that they then share with the rest of us."

Sexuality

"But I would like to discuss Rumi's poetry," Medina said. "Rumi used words of romantic, sexual loving to describe his 'courting' of God. In constantly yearning for his Beloved—God, he compared it to our human loving to get his point across. He seemed to relish and celebrate our own sexual loving as a human gift, a joy of living."

Sonya brightened and told us that her Hindu heritage included detailed explorations of sexuality in the "Kamasutra" and "Vatsyayana" writings. She added, "The tenth century BC Khajuraho Temple is world famous for the sexually explicit statues that adorn the outside of the temple."

Todd commented that Buddhism includes extensive literature on Tantric sexual teachings.

Rachael looked at me and asked, "Jo, are you familiar with the book of Solomon in your Old Testament—our Torah?"

"No, I'm not."

She grinned, "That whole book celebrates the lovers, the physical enticements of sexual love. It's told through stories full of fruits and flowers and playful animals, but doesn't screen the strong, irresistible attraction between lovers. Today, sexual intimacy is actually encouraged as part of our Jewish family Sabbath."

We wondered why human sexuality was historically celebrated within the spiritual world but the attitude supporting its joy and reverence had gradually declined.

I told them of having read that, as early Christianity gained momentum and power, Rome decided to incorporate it as its official religion, thereby gaining some control over the flourishing faith. The Greco-Roman philosophy of human sexuality as carnal and crude then began to pervade that belief system. Because of their pagan history, the Celtic branch of Christianity, as practiced in the British Isles—especially Ireland—was still celebrating nature and procreation with their faith. But, I suggested that gradually, sexuality was sanitized out of the Christian religion as the Roman church became the dominant authority.

Medina added confirmation that as this happened, much of the world moved toward the powerful patriarchal influence. She said, "In too many cultures, there followed a systematic suppression of the 'divine feminine'. The female—the creative mother, the abundant, integrated, feminine part of life—was slowly demoted, restrained, and degraded."

We agreed that Muhammad and Buddha and the Jewish Jesus supported the female as valuable and a compliment to the male, but often, their messages were overshadowed by the patriarchal cultural trend.

We all thanked Medina for educating us into the Muslim and Sufi religions and cultures and I added, "Having this information more well-known would be a good start toward breaking down the ignorance-based fear and hatred that many have of Muslims, the xenophobia that contaminates our western world."

Finally, Rachael turned to Medina, "The Arab, Palestinian and Israeli wars are so fresh on my mind, so painful to me because I have family in Israel. My emotions overtook my common sense. I'm so sorry for my outburst. Thank you for giving me a more balanced perspective. It helps so much."

She continued, "More than your words, your actions *demonstrated* your Muslim beliefs. You just gave us the best example of living in peace that we could have witnessed. Instead of reacting to me—to my harsh words—you were silent and then tried to explain your Muslim religion while not withdrawing your affection for me. I can feel your love and I thank you."

---

7 Buenos Aires

Buenos Aires, Argentina is a beautiful international city of lovely parks, a botanical garden, an incredible zoo, and most famous, the City of the Dead.

Our tour group assembled for brunch in a private room of the hotel restaurant. The menus were printed in French and Spanish. No English. This communication barrier was averted because Rachael, who held a doctorate in French, translated for us. No unwelcome surprises for breakfast.

Extraterrestrial Visits

Jack stepped to the podium and began to speak and show pictures of convincing evidence of "Extraterrestrial visits." He had extensive knowledge on the subject and spoke with much passion about how the archeological and scientific world simply would not acknowledge the evidence as proof.

"The site for discussion is Puma Punku," he said. "It means 'Gate of the Lions' in the native tongue. Situated on a 13,000 foot high barren plateau in remote Bolivia, the site is incredibly difficult to visit.

"On that barren highland can be found precisely *straight-edged* blocks of granite, andesite and diorite. Diorite is a grayish-green plutonic rock of enormous hardness, density and resistance. The gigantic, extremely heavy blocks are scattered about in a confused chaos, but it is still possible to sense their original arrangement. The monoliths are dressed, cut and polished with a precision that can *usually* only be achieved in a workshop stacked with high-tech machines, hard-steel milling tools, and drills."

He banged his fist on the podium to emphasize, "And yet, rectangular grooves cut deep into the monoliths were straight as a ruler and each precisely the same. Some of these monstrous stones were united into structures that entirely elude reconstruction today." All during the lecture we examined photos and architectural renderings of the stones. It seemed as though they all originally fit together like very complicated Lego blocks.

Jack went on, "There were no shavings or evidence of the waste of construction. Those stones were *moved there* and the main platforms, when combined as originally built, were the size of an eleven story house. No technology today can do that. No known ancient civilization had that technology either. No explanation works, except extraterrestrial intervention!

"The native Aymara Indian tradition has maintained for millennia that these structures were built by gods in a single long night. According to folklore, these gods could fly, and eventually they destroyed their own work by lifting it up into the air, turning it upside down and letting it fall." In the photographs, the residual chaos does look like it resulted from some such violent act.

After breakfast, with Jack's astounding lecture over, we took a short break. As I walked up the stairs, there was that feeling again—the sense of how short our lives are compared to the thousands of years those precisely crafted stones had lain on that barren plateau... And the extra-terrestrials who made them... *What were they like, those ETs? They had all that massive technology and what else? I wonder what we might have in common with them. Sonya says we are magnificent beings; are they also?*

Very soon we assembled in the lobby to walk to the infamous "City of the Dead". I was so anxious to get started that I slipped out the side door and leaned forward, out into the alleyway, trying to see the city streets.

With an abrupt shock, I felt a "*plop*" on the crown of my head and *warm* liquid started to travel down my hair and scalp. "Yuuuuuuk Eeeeeew! Pigeons!" Pitiful whining escaped from my lips.

Todd heard the distress and, spotting the cause, grabbed some tissue to come to the rescue. "Hold still," he pleaded. I was squirming in disgust. Finally the "poop" was mostly cleaned up and I returned to my normal state of mind in time to notice that the other tour members, including Jack, had really enjoyed the show. Stiff with embarrassment, I thanked Todd for the rescue. Eventually, the episode became one of our favorite stories of the trip... eventually.

As we walked along the lovely old European-flavored streets to our destination, Rachael admitted, "Buenos Aires is not one of my favorite cities because I am a Jew and Nazi leaders and torturers were allowed to immigrate here, to live out normal lives after World War II."

A wistful look settled on her face and I asked, "What's wrong?"

She admitted she was lonely for her elderly husband who had been her lifetime traveling companion and had recently become too frail to travel. This trip was scheduled before his health faltered and he had insisted that she go without him. She said, "I automatically want to share any new discoveries with him. It's so strange to be doing this alone."

Then her face lit up as she said, "His beautiful mind is as sharp as it always was, though—inquisitive, probing the meaning in everything. I'll bring all of this to him and we'll enjoy it, examine it together."

Draping my arm around her shoulder I said, "We're a poor substitute for your husband, but your new friends here will share as much as we can with you. Let me take pictures when something of interest comes up so you can take the images home to him."

The City of the Dead

The City of the Dead, also known as Recoleta Cemetery, sits behind solid walls and is in fact, a kind of city. There are street signs for the tiny roads lined with trees, park benches and street lights. Argentine history is laid to rest among mausoleums, crypts and little miniature cathedrals.

Eva Peron is the most famous resident and following our street map we discovered her miniature stone chapel with peaked slate roof. We peered into the glass door and windows. It was rumored that her remains were actually buried under the street in front of the chapel, to deter grave robbers.

Wandering on to other interesting small memorials, we could see coffins inside through broken windows and spider webs, which only added to the eeriness of the setting.

One narrow lane was especially spooky with large overhanging trees blocking the light. It was lined with taller, grey stone ancient crypts. Jack told us that a ghost was frequently seen on that street. We huddled a little tighter together and when he told us of an open crypt that we were allowed to explore, most of us passed on that opportunity.

Amazingly, the three silver haired ladies dared each other to enter. They worked up their courage to hesitantly creep down the steps into the dark building. The rest of us exchanged mixed glances—part disbelief, part admiration.

Abruptly, horrible screams erupted! The women frantically tumbled over each other to get out. Jack caught one as she tripped on the steps. *He had set it all up!* In a coffin, hidden under a dusty blanket, his accomplice had exploded out just as the women entered the little room. I realized that he was having great fun with those three women and they loved it... eventually.

I asked Rachael to pose with the three women and Jack so she could take that story home.

After we explored the graveyard, Sonya and I rested on a convenient stone bench and I shared a memory of a "funny" funeral I had attended.

"A flamboyant, 'life of the party' woman was being buried. After the service, family and friends filed out of the 1940's stone chapel situated conveniently in the middle of the graveyard. We watched as the casket was rolled out the door, across the road, and then lifted into the back door of a waiting black hearse.

"Everyone went to their cars and waited for the hearse to lead the usual procession about four blocks to the graveside. Nothing happened. I saw one of the family members out in the street, pointing and shouting. Eventually, a bright red pickup truck passed us, *carrying the casket!* The deceased's grown son and daughter were perched on the tailgate with arms locked, *holding mama in the truck!*

"Quite puzzled but amused, we all fell into the procession behind the truck and diligently followed to the graveside. Passing another tiny graveside ceremony in progress, we noticed the participants craned their necks around and stared with open mouths at our funeral line. I wondered if they thought we got the 'economy package'.

"After the *very* brief graveside service, the mystery was solved when we found that the hearse keys had gone missing, and they had to improvise! I told the family that the spirit of the deceased woman probably hid the keys to ensure a 'show stopping exit'."

Sonya chuckled as we joined the group for our return.

The Labyrinth

Continuing the tour, we passed an impressive cathedral where Jack pointed out a labyrinth we could visit, and "walk" if we chose. About ten of us were interested and the rest could easily find their way back the short distance to the hotel, so Jack decided to walk it with us. He explained that the complicated pattern of curvaceous paths had one way in and back out again and that the mysterious labyrinths had been found near cathedrals all over Europe, from medieval times. It is a popular meditative practice to wander through a labyrinth in silence.

I was impatient to begin the walk, as each of us waited at the entrance. We made sure there was at least three minutes between us, and then began to walk a distance behind the person in front. Flat paver stones were easy to navigate, nestled between low miniature "monkey grass." Vaguely conscious of others near me moving along their own part of the path, I knew that these labyrinths were considered a metaphor for life—a path of life—if experienced deeply.

The center of the pattern was the goal to attain and it was slightly frustrating to find oneself almost there, only to realize that the path would inexplicably take off to explore another direction. With complicated weavings in and out, it would finally turn back toward the center again. I saw how each of us was following the same path but experiencing it differently, at separate times. Occasionally two people would seem to meet at a spot even though on different parts of the path.

I turned a corner to find Jack facing me and he paused briefly. I too, stopped and silently looked at him. We contemplated each other without distraction for a brief, breathless moment. Then he bowed slightly as if to say, "It's your call. Go on, or stay a while." I nodded an acknowledgement, smiled and moved on.

Once the center was attained, one could pause a bit or go on to navigate the return path out. Jack's presence had flooded my senses and I saw an option in life where our paths might converge.

The group eventually straggled out of the labyrinth and returned the two blocks to the hotel. Jack was gone when I finished, so I looked forward to my room and a chance to shower. It was heavenly to finally wash my hair of the bird poop I received on the path that the bird and I had shared… for just a moment in time.

Back in our room, Sonya stole a few minutes to snuggle in her bed and record her thoughts on her computer.

I was very enthusiastic about her book and wanted to help. "Why don't you include the story of the graveyard today? Embellish your book with more stories." Secure in her love, I felt privileged to offer my advice. "I noticed that the very first of your book is your personal, chronological history. It doesn't seem to be written with as much excitement and energy as the rest of your manuscript. It's just one fact after another, kinda boring. Do you think you could change that part up so it isn't so, well…" (I searched for another word but sadly used the same rude word) "…*boring?*"

Sonya looked at me, for the first time in our friendship, with a hard stare. She abruptly closed her laptop and silently began to dress for the evening. That was to be the last time she would share her book with me.

Tango

The next adventure on our agenda was to visit an Argentine Tango supper club, one of the events I had been looking forward to.

The Argentine Tango! World famous and much admired, it was the dance I had always wished for on *Dancing with the Stars,* my favorite show on television.

At the turn of the century, after the restrained, straight-laced cultural norm of the Victorian era, "Tangomania" swept through the world like a cultural tornado. New York, London and Paris were the epicenters of the storm. Tango was scandalous!

On the outskirts of Bueno Aires, the dance had gestated in the lower classes—the disenfranchised, the washer women, laborers, immigrants, and even the pimps and their prostitutes. This Tango told of their hard lives, the negative and positive raw emotions of passionate sexual attraction exposed through dance. Also exposed were the women, themselves, having dropped their heavy cumbersome clothing to slip into more form-fitting, body-revealing attire. Tango was a dance of the streets, an authentic dance of their lives.

In the 1980's, ballroom dancing, and especially the Tango, was an undeveloped passion of mine. So my husband and I took lessons and tried to learn the Tango. The dance originally portrayed a story of discord and emotional tension between the romantic partners. This turmoil was always followed by make-up passionate sexual displays. It seems today, that the angry, distressed side of Tango has slipped out of fashion. But the romance and raw sexual attraction between partners is enhanced even more, and the dance has evolved to a very passionate and sometimes tender display.

I hope this is an indication that we are evolving, like the dance, into having less discord in our relationships.

After my husband and I had taken lessons together, I realized formal dancing was not his talent. He had good moves, but the counting and required steps took his joy away. So we did our college swing dance at parties and a little two-step here and there. I lived vicariously by watching the dances on television, hoping for good tangos. The steps were still in my mind, but rusty.

The supper club called for a special dress and, diving into the suitcase, I retrieved the satin skirt with a deep, leg-exposing side slit that was perfect for the Argentine Tango. The tour schedule had listed a Tango club on our agenda and that skirt was my first purchase, in preparation for the trip.

That night at the club we were escorted to a lovely dance floor surrounded by tables that sat on graduated levels, elevated for good viewing. Snacking on light food and drinks, we leaned forward to enjoy the show.

The professional dancers began to entertain splendidly. It was the tango I had longed for, the "National Treasure of Argentina": a dance of passionate love, repeated again and again, in different arrangements and with different costumed dancers, but telling the same old human story of passionate sexual energy. There was a break and then the dancers came into the audience and chose people to come and dance with them.

Glory of glories, I was chosen, although not by a mysterious dark stranger, but a skinny man with big ears and prominent Adam's apple. He became just the right partner when I realized his gentle lead and instructions brought out my old, barely-remembered steps and moves. Gradually, bit by bit, my confidence grew and, just when I really began to *dance*, it was over. He escorted me back to the table and chose another lucky woman, just as he knew he should do.

But, to my dismay, there stood Jack by my chair, grinning and extending his hand to dance.

Flushed with the excitement of the tango, I felt myself blanch with fear. *Would I embarrass myself? Would I look foolish?* The love of the music pulsing all around and his gentle pulling on my hand urged me toward the dance floor. He carefully led me into the dance and we *became* the tango, pulsing and throbbing, twisting and bending, showing the opposing emotions of love and resistance that *are* the tango.

The thought flew through my mind: *This is one of the highlights of my entire life. When I am old and looking back, this will be the scene of one of my greatest joys.*

The Tango requires a closeness of bodies. With my head correctly nestled into the hollow between his neck and shoulder and his arm completely enfolding my back, we were glued together. There was "fire in the hole!"

After three dances we were breathless. He escorted me back toward my seat but unexpectedly pulled me further around a corner to a hidden alcove in the hall. There he pressed us against the wall. We melded together as in the dance, while he covered my mouth with kisses.

I was overwhelmed with the intensity of my response but conscious of being discovered, we separated—too quickly. His room key materialized in my hand, and he was gone.

It's been sooo long since I've felt this! I thought, leaning against the wall. I waited for a few moments until my heart calmed down and my legs stopped shaking, then I returned to my seat.

The rest of the show was a blur due to the jumble of internal arguments. *Should I? He's a player. Would I be a fool? Would I feel humiliated later, like one of the harem? But ohhh… how I want this— at last there is passion in my life, however brief.*

One of the harem? Well darn it—it's my turn with the Sheik!

A short trip to the room to freshen up and then I was tapping timidly on his door. Before there was time to use the key the door swung open and he scooped me into the darkened room and shut the door behind us. He pressed me against that door with his whole body.

Kisses and kisses reigned across my face, ears, neck and mouth. Each breast was gently explored and then he drove his body firmly against me again. His insistent "wanting" and determined pursuit inflamed my mind even more than the actions of his hands or body.

Our breathing became rapid, almost gasping.

With his knee, he slid my thighs apart and waded in deeper. Unexpectedly, the most amazing thing happened! Because his hips moved slowly side to side, our most sensitive parts were drawn to each other and the sexual tension swelled, inflamed, higher and stronger—*this has to be the top*—then even higher, until *Glory of Glories,* standing absolutely straight up—against that hall door— fully clothed—I had the strongest orgasm imaginable. "Oh God... Oh my God! Oh my good God!" escaped from my lips at the peak of the pleasure.

Again the shaking legs betrayed me, and he supported and guided me to the bed. The discarding of clothes allowed us to catch our breath, then a condom appeared from his pocket.

Leaning me back, he gave what I most wanted in the world at that moment. I lost track of everything but the two of us, moving as one—one entity—a giving, receiving, sharing entity.

Some people say that the combined experience of sexual orgasm— the complete communication of the two bodies—and the mental state which is truly "out of body"—is the closest we on earth can get to the experience of heaven. I agree.

Later, we snuggled up together and just enjoyed the silence, the recovery, the peace.

After a while I felt ready to leave him and as he walked me to that precious door he asked, "Are you okay?"

"Better than okay." I grinned in the dark.

He gave parting kisses on the back of my neck, squeezes on my arms, hugs from behind, a muffled "You are an amazing woman," spoken from deep in the curve of my neck and I opened that door and left.

Sonya seemed to be sleeping so I enjoyed a lovely hot shower, and then drifted off into a deep sleep with no thoughts, just blissful contentment, and with a smile on my recently ravaged lips.

I missed a similar smile on Sonya's face.

The next day as we waited to board the plane to Lima, Peru, I shared a brief, intimate glance with Jack and then the tour group, including several women, had him again.

I watched him mixing and mingling, in his element, his bliss.

Okay, I thought. *Where does this situation leave me now? Jack has no idea who I really am. There's no room for exploring each other in depth. But he did not "use me". We shared each other. He broke open my Joy by allowing me to really, totally dance the Tango and to re-connect with my own sexuality. Neither of us is married, so no one was hurt or betrayed. It was a gift.*

Ironically, I recognized in Jack my own past weakness; the urge to validate his sense of self through being pursued by the women that he admired. It made me feel a strange sort of "kinship" with him—a tenderness.

In my youth it would have seemed very important that Jack still pursue me, *prefer* me, over any other woman. With his barnyard rooster mentality, that attitude could only bring me pain. But, still vulnerable after all these years, my ego called out—wanting to be appreciated, desired.

Here I was, a mature woman with long abstinence from this particular magnetic pull but, like the alcoholic after the first sip of wine, I recognized that rush, that craving, the marvelous flush of sexual attraction. I was hooked again.

I think one of the ultimate gifts of human life is the opportunity to experience romantic sexual love. But perhaps this precious gift should come with an indelible warning label:

USE WITH CAUTION.
MAY BE HAZARDOUS TO YOUR MENTAL HEALTH.

TAOISM *"Think not that I would teach you to banish love from your heart; for that would be to go against the Tao. Love what you love, and be not misled by the thought that love is a hindrance which holds you in bondage. To banish love from your heart would be a mad and earthly action, and would put you further away from the Tao than you have ever been."*

Wu Wei, chapter I

---

8 Jack

Finally! That Jo McCrae was a hard one to get alone. She and Sonya seemed to attract folks to them like magnets. After a few glimpses of her during the day at Iguazu and then during his talk that night—they just vanished. He thought he saw another woman and the big blonde man with them talking animatedly, and then "poof." Gone.

On the plane to Buenos Aires their group of five sat together, deep in conversation. He'd listened in on the way to the bathroom and heard Sufi religious practices being discussed. On the way back it was Tantric sex! If there'd been an empty seat close to them, he would have slid into it. But there wasn't one.

The same thing happened in Buenos Aires. He chuckled at the memory of Jo's melt-down in the hotel lobby over a little pigeon poop. Even then, the big blonde guy—what was his name? Todd— jumped right in to rescue her. *I might have had some competition there for her affections, if I hadn't quickly "cut in."*

That practical ghost joke at the City of the Dead was a success, but he never dreamed the three old ladies would be the ones to take the bait. When they started down the stairs, he had nearly panicked—imagining a broken hip or two in the stampede he'd set off. He had hovered at the door with his arms out wide and the first one fell into them, grabbing him so hard he had bruises to show for it. The other two narrowly averted a calamity, Thank God!

Ironically, those three were becoming his best fans. Their approval warmed his heart because it felt a little like the love and affection he used to receive from his mother, before Alzheimer's took that away.

Who would have guessed that the Tango would provide the perfect opening with Jo? When she got a chance to dance, he watched as she moved through initial hesitancy and on into thoroughly expressing the Tango. Perfect. He *loved* the Tango.

It was uncanny how their dancing together was so effortless— came so naturally to them both. It was almost as if they were able to read each other's minds—anticipate each next move.

That was *really fun*. He couldn't remember another partner who melded into him, whose body almost became an extension

"All deeds originate in the heart. All good acts begin in the heart and are completed too, in the heart. The heart's in-most recess is the very spot where there is Heaven and where there is Hell."

Yin Chih Wen

---

9 Santiago, Chile

New wings would lift us from the grey Atlantic Ocean over jagged, snow-dusted Andes Mountains to the blue Pacific Ocean and drop us onto the narrow sliver of coastline that is Chile. While we waited to board, Mildred left her loyal companions to join me.

I involuntarily shuddered, having just come from what she would call "a bed of fornication."

"Jo, may I sit with you on this next plane to Chile?"

I agreed to be her seatmate while suspecting I was to be the recipient of "witnessing for Jesus."

My friends rolled their eyes at me in sympathy and found other places to sit.

All was quiet for several minutes after we settled in seats far to the back of the plane. (I couldn't risk another tirade out in the middle of everyone.)

Mildred leaned toward me and almost whispered, "I like you Jo. What I want to say is hard for me. If I don't have righteous indignation to fire me up, I'm actually shy."

Wow! I thought, *that's a perceptive observation on her part.*

Mildred stretched a pointing finger out at the people on the plane. "You see all these people? We're all *sinners,* every one of us. Born in original sin and blundering into more and more sins all our lives. I'm one of the worst!"

She had my full attention.

"Yes I *am.* Before my marriage I had three lovers and I even slept with my husband two years before we were married." She looked at me with intensity. "Those were *sins.* It says so in the Bible.

"I could finally see the harm of what I was doing—the example I was living. My actions could encourage an innocent person who was considering the same choices—a girl who might give in and end up pregnant.

"I didn't care about it before… but I do now. I came to believe in Jesus and ended up lugging around a ton of guilt over my past—couldn't stand it anymore.

"We have a fabulous choir at our church and one night, the words of those old hymns we were singing suddenly seemed to sink right into my heart. The words were my words—the sorrows, my sorrows—the love and forgiveness—my release.

"Down at the altar on a Sunday night, those sins, those 'indelible' sins, were washed white as snow in an instant!

"Oh," she added, "and because of that, I came to know Jesus and He talks to me and tells me He loves me and I am His. When I'm alone and scared, I can tell Him *anything* and He calms me down. He is my ticket to heaven, no matter what I have done or might do. "*He has saved me from hell.*"

I got it! Instead of arguing with her that she wasn't a sinner in need of saving, originally or now—as was *my* belief and my first impulse—I got it. *Her belief* had saved her, just like the woman in the Bible who was healed just by touching the robe of Jesus—saved because she believed. She had the "Peace of God that surpasses understanding" just like all those other generations of people. And in her church service, she had the *experience* of God through Jesus, that same experience I was craving from *my* church services.

Another realization appeared on my spiritual horizon. That Voice that speaks to her in the night—that compassionate, unconditionally loving Voice she calls Jesus—is the same as my personal comforter, my Voice, that Voice of the past that always sustained me, although currently, the Voice was dim because of my own ambivalence and doubts. Some people call it Jesus, some call it Holy Spirit and some have other names for it.

I don't know what to call It. I once asked, "What do I call You?" The response came, "*I don't care what you call Me. Just call Me!*"

Mildred reached out and captured my hand to pull my wandering attention back. "Jo, you're a precious child of God with your own special purpose. Created by God—and will be fulfilled by Him— guided by His Word." She finally got to her pitch—in my face and intense—"Do you have a personal relationship with Jesus Christ?"

I thought for a moment and realized, *Yes...! I do!* Or at least I had, and somehow knew I would hear it again. "Hallelujah!"

Mildred looked me in the eyes and saw that I spoke the truth. I think, in that moment, she recognized me as a sister with the same feminine, sensual nature as her own.

"That Jack is on your trail, Jo. He wants you *bad.*" She stretched her hand toward my heart and gently tapped my chest. "But you have Jesus in your heart. You'll be all right."

God had spoken to me in the strangest way, dressed in the costume of Mildred, my new friend.

Santiago

We came at Easter and here in Chile, it is celebrated in the fall. Similar to California, there were the same forests of tall fir and spruce trees, the same wide green "bread basket" valley nestled against mountains. Even the same produce—grapes, wine and blueberries. "Upside down", the further south you go, the colder it gets.

Five million people live in Santiago, tucked among modern skyscrapers and buildings of European (especially French) architecture and built in the late 19th and early 20th centuries.

The air quality during our tour was pretty grim. A pocket of brown and stagnant atmosphere hovered over the city, caught between low foothills on the coast and the mountains beyond the valley. Even the smog of California was here.

An ordinance allowed private cars, with license plates ending in an even number, to drive one day and odd-numbered ones the next. Ironically, the prolific diesel buses—pumping black smoke— daily performed a four wheeled "roller derby," knocking off the competition by passing a front bus and racing to the next customers.

We were surprised to see a fire truck cruising around the streets full of grown boys happily hanging on. It seems the new graduates from high school are required to give one year to the city as firefighters and they were engaged in their training sessions.

Several years ago, the military rule in Chile was overthrown after a terrible period of domination and the frequent "disappearing" of people who were perceived to be threats to the government. Democracy is in place now and has sported as many as twenty political parties at one time. Our group concluded that someone was doing something right because the city was spotlessly clean. No litter. The modern subways reminded me of a kitchen—gleaming white tiles, brightly lit and again, no trash, not even a chewing gum wrapper.

Easter Eve, a rippling thrill of ooohs and ahhhs moved through the crowd.

The event was over in only a minute or two. Lights were turned back on and the restaurant owner stood up and tapped his fork on a wine glass, to get everyone's attention. "In the morning it is Easter Sunday and I want to rejoice with you all that Jesus arose out of the grave just like that moon. He loved us and showed us there *is* life after death. Thanks be to God... A bus will be outside your hotel lobby at 5:30 tomorrow morning for those who would like to attend our Easter Sunrise Service on the beach."

He then walked out to the little dance floor and motioned for our pretty dark haired guide. They performed what appeared to be a national folk dance. The owner portrayed a very proper, gentlemanly "rooster" and our pretty guide played the flirting flitting "hen" and waved a handkerchief invitingly during their "courtship."

When they were finished, the guide pulled Jack to the dance floor to teach *him* the dance and we enjoyed his struggle to learn. But I knew that rooster could *dance* and sure enough, he adopted the role of a rather more insistent, hotly pursuing, feathered Romeo. He then expanded the act to include the whole restaurant and received a rousing applause.

I was aware of Jack all that evening. My body tracked the position of his body like a GPS. My mind stayed busily involved in the tour events and interplay with people, enjoying it all but, Jack was like a magnet pulling at me. I wanted to be near him—lock eyes with him—touch his shoulder as I passed, to appease the hunger I felt for his presence.

The establishment must have been serving several Pisco Sours because the customers, inspired by Jack's "cocky" demonstration, got a little crazy.

One attractive woman tourist decided to sit on almost every male lap in the restaurant, with the pretense of having her picture taken to commemorate the evening. The men happily obliged and Jack got an especially long "sit."

I watched as he dropped his hands to her hips and *squeezed*. She squealed happily and twisted around in his lap until she could kiss him on the cheek, "accidentally" pressing an ample breast into his chest. Reluctantly, she rose from his lap and, as she rounded our end of the room, Rachael dryly asked, "How many laps have you made?"

My mind screamed, *Damn! Jack really is a playboy— an enthusiastic, fully participating, rutting stag. This relationship I so lustily jumped into is a dead end."*

So I decided to fight it. I thought, *I can cool the fire in me, control myself. I have to back up before he romances the next woman right in front of me and I'm left feeling humiliated.*

The party broke up and on the bus back to the hotel, we friends discussed attending the early morning Easter service.

Rachael looked at us and said somewhat dejectedly, "You Christians probably don't want me to attend, since you think of us Jews as 'Christ killers'."

Horrified, I said, "Christ killers?"

She muttered, "Lots of Christians call Jews that, because it was the Jews who turned Jesus over to the Romans for crucifixion."

I was hurt. "Well *I* don't," I countered, "and I'm amazed you'd lump me into such a category. I'm grateful for the Jewish heritage that produced Jesus. The Hebrew people loved Jesus and still do. Prophets of reform were seldom treated well. Muhammad even had to run for his life to the city of Medina."

Our Medina laughed and jokingly said, "Well then, I guess I'm going to the Easter service with all you 'infidels'. By the way, do you know what the real meaning of the word 'infidel' is...? It translates to 'one who lacks thankfulness'. But, I do feel quite comfortable at your Christian service because Muslims honor Jesus as one of our four most important prophets and some of us believe he *was* the Messiah!"

"What did you just say? The Messiah?" I couldn't believe it.

She nodded. I thought I saw her eyes fill with tears. She spoke in a tender loving voice when she said, "We believe Jesus didn't die on the cross. God took him Home while he was still alive in his body and we are waiting for him to come back to save the world. He's *alive.*"

I was flabbergasted! How could we *not know* that Jesus was so important to Islam?

Rachael wasn't herself. I had noticed that she seemed uncharacteristically preoccupied throughout the dinner party. Slipping into the seat next to her on the return bus, I tried to understand what was wrong.

Rachael admitted that something was indeed bothering her. She had received a call from her divorced daughter who shared one more episode in the ongoing alcoholic, codependent saga involving a long-time boyfriend. He had become violent and she had to be hospitalized due to a concussion she suffered from being shoved into a wall.

"Nothing I have ever said or done has made any difference and actually just made it worse," she said. "My daughter is addicted to the toxic relationship. This anger I feel toward her boyfriend is totally consuming me! I don't know what to do with it."

"Why don't you come to our room when the bus drops us off?" I asked. "You need to talk it out."

CHRISTIAN *"Relation is the essence of everything that exists."*

Meister Eckart

---

10 Challenges We Plan Before Birth

Sonya wanted another get-together, and by the time we got to our hotel room the group had swelled to five again.

I whispered to Rachael that I'd like to talk about the challenges of dealing with anger but that I'd only talk in generalities—I wouldn't reveal her secret.

Starting the discussion, I admitted struggling with debilitating anger at different times in my life. Two experiences gave me new insights in coping with these seemingly unbearable emotions.

"The first eye-opening example was the life experience of a friend. This woman was a psychologist whose son, Daniel, a headstrong boy, battled depression all his life and was forever in trouble with drugs, alcohol and jail. He grew up and was living in California. She went to his college graduation and saw that he was happier and less depressed so she went home comforted.

"*Then he killed himself shortly after she left.* She nose-dived into depression and grief—mentally beating herself up for not suspecting anything—not *doing* anything. Non-functional, she closed her practice and went into seclusion for nearly two years.

"After that time, she tried to pick herself up and get on with her life. Not having much success, she went to a meditation workshop to see if that would help. As she sat in meditation she was given a 'vision'.

"In her vision, she was surrounded by several strangely familiar, extremely nurturing and loving people. One of them said to her, '*Daniel's incarnation was a difficult one. We gave him to you because you were strong and could bear it—and you did. Thank you.*'

"When she could see a wider perspective and the greater plan of Daniel's life, she started on the road to recovery. She was able to release the anger at herself and guilt that had held her captive for so long.

"The second mind-changing example was a hypnotherapy client that I read about in one of Dolores Cannon's books. This woman, when regressed, remembered a past life in Ireland. She was the very poor mother of six kids and married to a drunken, abusive husband.

"Quite admirably, she was able to survive that very difficult life and to raise and care for her children well. When she died, she went to the *other side* and back to her *soul group,* where they all cheered her victory over such a hard incarnation.

"On the front row was her *husband,* who in actuality was her dear friend that had only agreed to play the part of the abuser in that past life in order for her soul to grow stronger."

Todd asked, "You said she went back to her 'soul group'—what is that?"

"I'm no expert on soul groups, but after reading so many accounts like that last one and from channeled information in Helen Greaves' *Testimony of Light,* I have adopted the idea.

"It seems that when we pass on, we eventually go back to our soul group, *one that we have always been a part of.* These souls are very close and incarnate together to play various roles for each other. These *pre-planned specific experiences* enable so much wonderful learning at the soul level.

"The possibility—the chance—that maybe the people who are bothering or mistreating me the most had agreed to do it *for me* and not *to me,* is a game changer. What if it is an agreement to help advance my soul growth? To view life from that perspective would bring me a much more peaceful existence, so I am trying to remember as each new 'opportunity' walks into my life, there's probably a lesson in every one of the suckers!"

Rachael just couldn't or wouldn't get her mind to turn that corner. As she told the group her daughter's story, her anger only escalated. She stood up and stalked around the cramped floor of the room in a rage.

We sat still in disbelief, afraid to move, shaken by the depth of her anger.

"I <u>know</u> this! It's part of my Jewish heritage, my teachings—God uses all things for good—but darn it, I refuse to give up my anger! I'm going to *have* my adolescent tantrum. If I don't let it out, I will explode! I seem to have been born with a short fuse—a volatile temper. Medina, you got a dose of it back on the plane to Buenos Aires. I'm sorry for that...

"All my life I have been driven to be perfect, to excel at *anything* I do. As a mother, my parenting skills had to be perfect and I was anxious about it all the time. Driven to succeed, my education was exemplary—my PhD provided a position teaching French and literature. That literature was a stretch—so *hard*. I studied even more to master the challenge. My personality called me to perfection and my Jewish DNA doubled it.

"We Jews are called to excellence, to live as 'a light unto the nations,' full of compassion and justice for the world. We should never waver in our intent—in the responsibility we carry as the 'chosen people'—the challenge we answered.

"We are taught that there is God in *all* facets of Creation. The people we judge as 'evil-doers' can be instruments of Divine Will. God uses *all* of creation for good.

"But it's not fair! I've tried to see the good in my daughter's relationship with a man who beats her so bad that she ends up in the hospital! I can't see the good in this at all. I want to break his knees with a baseball bat!"

Exhausted, she flopped on the bed and burst into tears.

I got up, wet a wash cloth and offered it to her during the silence that stretched out after her outburst.

Todd tentatively spoke, "When someone is 'renting space in my brain' and won't let go, I say a slightly altered version of the 'Prayer of Protection' for that person, over and over... *even while not wanting to do it*. For me, it melts the anger away."

He quoted the prayer,
>"The light of God surrounds_____ (the jerk)
>The love of God enfolds _____ (the jerk)
>The power of God protects _____ (the jerk)
>The presence of God watches over _____ (the jerk)
>Wherever (the jerk) is, GOD IS, and all is well."

Todd went on to say, "I was told to pray for the person who angered me, but I couldn't find a way to be *willing* to do it. So this prayer somehow does it for me, and 'the Jerk' becomes another *child of God, and God's responsibility to fix, **not mine**.*"

Rachael smiled through her tears and said, "I think I can manage that one. I'll especially enjoy saying 'the Jerk' part!"

Sonya quietly said, "I'm so sorry for your painful situation Rachael. But I think the souls playing those villain roles—those evil-doers—must experience pain and difficulties too. I believe that sometimes the degree of pain inflicted *outside,* on others, is a measure of the pain they endure *inside* themselves."

"Hey! That's another way of finding forgiveness for the 'Jerks', I said. "Hadn't ever considered the mental challenges *they* face."

Ho'oponopono

After a bit, I asked, "Has anyone ever heard of Ho'oponopono?"

"Ho o what oh?" asked Medina.

"It sounds like 'ho-o-pono-pono'", I explained. "It's an ancient Hawaiian healing method—a practice of forgiveness and reconciliation. A modern version was introduced by Dr. Ihalekala Hew Len. The concept he put into action is to take 100% *responsibility for everyone's actions, not **only** for one's own!*"

Medina exclaimed, "Jo, you have finally gone too far for me. I am not going there! *I am responsible for myself and my own actions and thoughts, period! Or maybe my kid's actions.*"

There was a generalized agreement of grunts around the room, but Rachael was silent.

Laughing, I said, "I know! That's what I thought until I read the documented story of how Dr. Hew Len applied his own theory, with amazing success! In this experiment, he worked at the Hawaii State Mental Hospital for four years and <u>never actually saw any of the patients</u>. The atmosphere of this institution was so toxic that other psychologists quit on a monthly basis and the staff called in sick and feared for their lives at work.

"For this reason, Dr. Hew Len preferred to have an office separate from the wards, where he reviewed the files of his patients. While he looked at each file, he would work on himself; as he worked on himself, the patient started to heal! Patients who had been shackled began to improve and were then permitted to walk around freely. Others, formerly on heavy medication, were tapered off it, and even those who were previously not expected to ever be set free were eventually released! The ward became a happy place but overstaffed, because the patient load kept shrinking and finally the entire ward was closed."

"What does that mean—Dr. Hew Len worked on himself?" asked Todd.

"He says he was healing the part of himself that created them." I replied. "He says that taking total responsibility for your life means that *you created all that you perceive in your life. The entire world you see is your creation and you are responsible for it.*

"I know, blaming others is much easier to do, but from this perspective, it is all about *healing yourself* and *loving yourself.* If you want to fix or cure anyone, you have to fix or cure yourself."

"So just *how* did he go about doing that?" challenged the skeptical Medina.

"He says he would just look at the patient's chart and repeat this Ho'oponopono prayer, over and over to himself.

> I'm sorry...
> Please forgive me...
> I love you...
> Thank you.

The gentle love—the total acceptance—healed the patient and himself. Dr. Hew Len says this meditation heals *you* and thereby heals the *world* because we are all connected, all part of the same consciousness.

"Ho'oponopono is another way of understanding what purpose we individuals have as members of humanity. I believe, knowingly or unknowingly, *we impact the Whole with our thoughts.* As we let go of toxic perceptions and energies, we open up a channel for the Divine to enter the world."

I finished my information about Ho'oponopono by saying, "I can't understand it, can't conceive of it, *but I swear it works.* I will lie in bed and instead of running those toxic stories about someone over and over in my head, I will focus on that person and say, 'I'm sorry. Please forgive me. I love you. Thank you'.

"I'll start by aiming it at the person, but somewhere in there it becomes love and forgiveness and gratitude for myself! This seems to open me up so that I can actually *feel God love me!* The hard knot that was my heart gradually melts and opens and *Love* pours in."

I got up and stretched and then it was my turn to pace back and forth in the restricted space. "The trick is to get to the point where I am *willing* to let that hateful attitude go. Sometimes, stubbornly staying in my festering anger and fuming over it is a necessary thing—replaying the saga over and over—chewing all the negative meat off that bone, savoring it!"

"Oh yeah, I know how that is," commented Todd.

Sonya agreed. "It's an inviting, self-perpetuating cycle that feeds on telling the story to sympathetic friends, isn't it? That *craving for affirmation, retribution and justification!*"

Medina jumped up and acted out her next words with a raised fist, "Inflaming larger and larger groups of people, it eventually brings on actual violence—violence justified by the thought that, 'We can't let that injustice go unpunished!' So the anger and its pain cycles on for generations."

"We don't search for a better way of living," I admitted, "until the pain pushes us over the brink personally or the cultural or national atrocities—like war—get intolerable globally." Unexpectedly, my mind flashed a phrase, unbidden, "Forgiveness in Jesus". *Where did that come from?*

I went on, "The possibility, the realization that my toxic thoughts are not just my own, but are somehow impacting and inflaming all of creation, does push me to let go of it sooner. If I'm that powerful as a part of the 'Oneness', then the responsibility I carry to send positive loving energy out into the world instead of dragging it down further, is huge!"

My friends studied me in silence, as they attempted to absorb this broader concept of self-responsibility into their minds. All but Rachael. Her head down, she appeared to be acknowledging this truth, but still unable to lay down her sword.

Todd muttered under his breath, "I thought I was doing good to just <u>think</u> black thoughts but not spit out the hateful words or act on them. I can't get away with *anything* anymore!"

Snickering surrounded him. We had heard… and empathized. Everyone got up and stretched and groaned, dreading the early morning wake-up call for the Easter Sunrise Service.

We were all going.

CHRISTIAN *"Split the wood—I am there; lift the stone and you will find me there."*

The Gospel of Thomas

---

11 Forgiveness in Jesus

We separated and everyone headed for bed, to snuggle down under the covers and digest the night's information. Some possibly explored pockets of unforgiveness, like a tongue probing into a rotting tooth cavity. Some might have initiated attempts at healing. Others probably chose to hang on to the "dis-ease" for a little longer but knew that, when they were ready, there might be a way out of it.

As I settled into my own bed, I realized that I had some work to do on my own little pocket of unforgiveness towards fundamentalist Christians, instead of preaching to friends. My God wouldn't need the sacrifice of His Son in order to forgive us and wouldn't damn us to hell for our sins. That was a source of dis-ease I carried about the Christian faith. My God who nurtures and forgives couldn't, wouldn't do that.

I believe that Jesus, *willingly and with forethought,* laid down His life for us, even though it was the hardest thing He would ever do. He could have saved Himself—*He was Jesus for Christ's sake!*

I believe it was His divine life plan, made before His birth, to help save mankind, to attempt to show us 'The Way'.

But a new insight, another way of looking at the issue occurred to me. The ancient Jewish belief of sacrifice to an angry God in order to appease Him was a well-established practice and seemed to get their prayers answered. But for the followers of Jesus, followers of 'The Way', Jesus' crucifixion was the last sacrifice needed. They were saved!

My quirky imagination dreamed up a scenario of God, up in Heaven, saying "Oh, Good Grief! If you insist on believing in the value of sacrifice then, here! Here is the last 'big' sacrifice and it takes care of everything... forever... OK?"

But then the next thought came. We *still* desperately need to be saved. Saved from fear and guilt and hatred of our brothers and the belief that we are alone, separate from God.

Jesus brought the message of Love and Forgiveness that saves us—*just the lessons we were wrestling with! He does save us after all, by example. What difference does it make which language or belief we use to get us to embrace the Christ consciousness? None!*

In the silence, a tiny thought grew in my mind. *What have you got left to forgive, Jo?*

Life is a Tango

I answered it. *Well... I guess... my husband. I need to forgive him for not giving me the love I wanted from him. He did the best he was capable of, with his addiction.*

A warm feeling softened my heart. The stony knot almost melted. Almost... There was something left.

What is it Lord?

Then I started weeping, as the painful realization dawned on me. *It's me Lord... It's me I have to forgive. For not being smart enough to 'fix' him. For all my angry hateful emotions that spilled out all over him, damaging his spirit even more. For all the things I did, or didn't do in my life that I am ashamed of.* Then I really sobbed, letting all that long-held guilt and blockage drain away with the tears.

A voice... "You did the best you knew how to do, precious Jo."

Jesus, Holy Spirit—my Presence, was back! Forgiving me—had always forgiven me. It was *my* forgiving me that had to happen!

A fear thought welled up. If I *actually* begin to believe that the Voice is Jesus, could truly <u>be the soul of Jesus</u>... then I might never be the same... I might look like those fundamentalist Christians I have judged. Then I snickered... then laughed out loud. I'd have to stop seeing myself as separate... because I had joined them!

So I laid it down... laid it all down on the altar of Jesus. I had my own "forgiveness in Jesus" that night.

Easter Sunrise Service

The early morning gathering in the lobby revealed disheveled, sleepy-eyed, unhappy folks, but I awoke with a new 'lightness' about me—a weight lifted. Jack was absent but the local guide got us on the bus.

We eventually found the beach, the site for the service. In the partial darkness, people with flashlights swarmed the area. Our little group scrambled to find a space to spread our hotel towels on the sand. Enveloped by large families, crying babies and rattling, excited, Spanish conversation, I wondered if we would understand a word of the service.

Over the commotion, we were soothed by the sound of crashing but calming waves, waves that gradually became visible with the earliest light. A strong, moist and salty ocean breeze flattened our hair back and bathed our eager faces. We could taste the salt on our lips.

Escalating excitement around us signaled the imminent sunrise and we turned away from the ocean to focus on the low hills to our east.

Just as the fiery orange sun burst upon the horizon, amid excited exclamations all around us, our ears were bathed in the sounds of the great *Hallelujah Chorus* being sung by a large, well-practiced choir. We heard the swelling sounds of harmonic voices, balanced and interactive male and female, each complementing and enhancing the other—the sum greater than the parts. And I felt my thankful, forgiven heart sing out, to join in the chorus.

Enveloped in the emotions of joy, celebration, and thanksgiving, goose bumps rose on our arms.

I was reminded of a teaching from *A Course in Miracles*.

"What is Heaven, but the song of gratitude, love and praise by all of Creation singing to its Creator?"

I also thought of Leonard Cohen's song of the same name, "Hallelujah." He sings of the pain in this life—the cuts and bruises and the brokenness endured during experiences of romantic love— while acknowledging and understanding the holiness of the whole divine process—the **Glory** of it all.

Hallelujah!

The spectacular sunrise and the choir proved to be the highlight of the service because the message *was* in Spanish. Happily, we found it to be brief and we soon stood up and gathered our towels and headed for the bus.

"I've got to get to a bathtub," grumbled Sonya, whose sari had allowed sand to go where sand should never be.

As we rode the bus back to the hotel in the tired silence of our group, I was carried away with my thoughts.

The beach we'd just left was probably empty again—back to the sounds of wind, surf and seagulls. I pictured the teaming groups of people as they had scrambled up from the sand to the street, trailing each other around obstacles of poles and bleachers and clumps of large families. They reminded me of rush hour traffic on the freeways of home. There, the cars performed a sort of dance, each moving independently, yielding or charging ahead, harmoniously as a rule. The rapid streams poured into fuller rivers, in perfect time with each other.

We bodies seemed to be moving through life, learning and changing, altering the steps into new patterns. Each turn in the road brought new partners, new opportunities, and new steps to attempt to learn.

Again I saw it as a dance, a dance of relationships with no insulating cars. This dance was up close and very personal—a Tango.

Our long, strenuous tour with its barrage of new sights, new information, change, and the constant challenge of coping with never-ending bus and plane rides, had a way of wearing us down. We were slowly dropping any façade we might have carried and the naked personalities of each one began to be visible.

To me it was a welcome sight, to see actions and reactions coming out that were so dearly, humbly human. I could see myself in every person, even Mildred.

At noon, we were to board a plane to Peru.

CHRISTIANITY *"For I am persuaded that neither death, nor life, nor angels, nor principalities, nor powers, nor things present, nor things to come, nor height, nor depth, nor any other creature, shall be able to separate us from the Love of God, which is in Christ Jesus our Lord."*

(Paul) Romans 8, 38-39

---

12 Lima, Peru

As we were milling around at the airport waiting for the latest plane, I noticed Sonya and Rachael intently bent over Sonya's laptop. Sonya asked, "What do you like best? I think it needs to be moved."

"Then do it. It's your book, your voice," said Rachael.

My heart wrenched with pain. Rachael, with her PhD in literature was a much better advisor to Sonya. Not only because of her education, but because she let Sonya write her own book.

I thought back over my bossy words, my presumption that I could say anything to Sonya and she would love and accept me. Apparently not. Our friendship now contained a hidden crack. All was well if the book was not mentioned, but I knew I couldn't ever repair the crack—get back her tender love. To be the recipient of such love and then fail it, cause it to be taken away, felt worse than never knowing that love at all.

When Todd asked to sit with me on the plane, I was grateful. We chose two seats in the back. It was noisy, but because of that, private. He took my hand and said, "I have a confession to make."

Puzzled, I just waited and looked at him.

His muscular shoulders hunched over in misery and with a mournful expression he said, "I'm gay."

Not being totally surprised, I grinned warmly and said, "So…?"

Grateful to be accepted and not judged, he spilled all the disease that was eating at his soul. "I was married for seven years to my best friend. She shared my hobbies and even work; both of us were registered nurses."

"But what started out good in the bedroom," he said, "withered away for me. For several years I was miserable—my soul yearned for that sexual thrill of attraction again, but it was always a man who caused the stirrings. It was hard, but I never cheated on my wife.

"Meanwhile, I watched her, this precious love of my life, as she shriveled and lost her feminine sense of self. Who was she, if not desirable? Even though it tore my heart to think of life without her, we divorced and after a while I saw her blossom and grow… Now she is happily remarried.

"I tried to explore being gay by playing the field but the superficial, lusty encounters left me embarrassed and empty inside." He grinned and threw up his hands in a shrug. "It appears I am a monogamous person."

Lunch came as a sack lunch and a drink. Eating prevented much conversation and we looked up as people stretched and walked back and forth to the restroom behind us. A short plump woman and a slender dark complexioned man from our tour had to wait beside our seats, so a conversation started up comparing our impressions of the experiences so far. They mentioned the parts they liked best and the man, Takil, spoke in an animated manner about the coming Peruvian experience. He thought it would be the best stop of our tour.

When the two of them had returned to their seats and the food was cleared away, Todd continued his story. "During a graduate class, an attractive, married professor initiated a romance with me, but the man would not contemplate leaving his loveless marriage and 'coming out' to the world and his profession. I finally faced the fact that there was no real future with him and had to end it.

"Broken hearted again, I embraced Buddhism and the Tao and... after two years... I'm single, celibate and shriveling on the vine." He smiled a weak smile, painted with chagrin.

I could hear the guilt-laden undertones, the same empty, lonely unhappiness that had propelled me toward this tour; the same desperate reaching out, straining for a life preserver.

We were getting tired of sitting, so we crawled out of our back seats to stretch and groan and visit the facilities. Then we paced to the front of the plane and back again several times.

As I passed Jack the first time, he looked at me and smiled. Then he looked at Todd behind me, and his eyes again sought my face with a questioning look. I reached out and squeezed his shoulder as I passed with a slight negative shake of my head, indicating "It's nothing." Despite that, when we passed him the second time, he looked down at a book, which was upside down.

Once again in our private nest in the back, I commented, "I think that we 'come in' with a set-up, a life situation perfectly designed for our growth. You came in with homosexual yearnings while dearly loving a woman; that's a hard road to travel. If you believe in reincarnation and karma, perhaps you lived a past life of condemning and persecuting homosexuals. So this time around you get to feel that—to *live* as one."

Todd stared at me, appalled. Then he appeared to chew on that concept a bit and begin to swallow and digest it, maybe using it to change him, help him to grow.

I tentatively admitted, "My life circumstances created a craving for love that also focused on men—craving the experience of relating to men—needing to *understand* them. I wanted their approval and validation.

"Sex is a wonderful opportunity for sharing love and intimacy, deep psychological intimacy, but sex can also be a substitute for true communication. One man I dearly loved would not open up, *could* not share himself with me that way. What I wanted was love—that exhilarating, infatuating *high* of freshly realized and then sustained love—sustained through shared intimacies, a baring of souls to one another. I guess all he wanted from me was to bare my body."

Todd squirmed in his seat. He said, "I blamed my professor for not 'coming out' for *me*, but I guess all *he* wanted was sex, too."

We looked at each other silently and then bowed our heads in the shared feeling of humiliation.

After a bit of silent contemplation, I continued with my past, "My mother died when I was three years old. She was birthing my brother, who also nearly died. My daddy fought valiantly at the hospital to save my brother and when they did come home to my grandmother's house, daddy drifted away from us into a cloud of alcoholism to combat the excruciating loss of his wife.

"I read years later, after I had worked through some of the pain, that little girls, *at three years of age,* form their sense of self, their *self-worth*, from their relationship with their fathers. Tragically, I had lost my daddy along with my mother at three. My self-confidence was annihilated.

"When I was five, he married 'the wicked step-mother,' who I eventually forgave and loved as much as she would let me. She organized and stabilized his life and got him back on track. Problem was, I was competition for his love, which he never gave *her* enough of either. So, although I believed that he loved me, he rarely hugged or touched or gave me his time and words of affirmation.

My father worked as a fireman for thirty years. Mid-career, he was promoted to the position of drill instructor—where he taught the young recruits how to climb tiny ladders far above the earth, and not to go down narrow alleys where the fire might drop a brick wall on them—to take care of *themselves* above all else, while honoring the powerful impulse to save the victims and the property. He eventually rose to the top—fire-chief. All through his career, he guarded his men and their safety. At his funeral, long after his retirement, so many firemen showed up that I was overwhelmed. I asked one, "My father has been retired for a long time. Why was it so important to come to his funeral?" The man held his hat respectfully in his hand and locked his eyes on mine to make me understand. He said, "He kept us *alive!*"

Todd commented, "It must have been something like going through a war together—there's a strong bond formed between those men, too."

"I think you're right," I said. "Then, as a child, I watched my father organize a scout troop of boys *my age* and follow them through the years as they grew, giving them camp-outs and teaching them about nature—which is what *I* craved. Those boys, now men, still talk about him with admiration and affection.

"He gave so much of himself to those boy scouts and to those firemen, but I felt like I didn't get my share. Why were they more interesting to him than me? There was emptiness in my soul. It was a 'set up.' What would I do with it? When old enough, I went 'boy-crazy'."

"Whoa! Boy crazy?"

"Yep! That old description fit me to a T. I became fascinated with the opposite sex—of course, puberty had a little something to do with that. After early years of craving outside validation, first from my father and then boys and on to men—suitable, intelligent men—I began to despair of finding *the one* because each man was not *it*. I would become infatuated, over and over, and soon it would fade away.

"I read a bit on sexual addiction once, and it was similar to my situation, but I was never drawn to the vast number of men that she was. This woman said she wasn't after the sex—actually sex became the anti-climax for her—because it was the chase itself, the 'high' of newly found infatuation that she was craving. She couldn't get enough validation to believe that she was admirable, desirable, *special*. There was an emptiness that could not be satisfied."

"Todd admitted, "I'm afraid there's the same addiction to be found in the gay population. I'm grateful that's not one of my problems."

It was amazing to see how similar we were, homosexual and heterosexual. I went on with my story. "Even though I couldn't find *'the one',* luckily, finally, he found me, but I still didn't trust myself. We waited three years to marry while I finished nursing school. By then, I could believe it would last. It did. I absolutely *knew* he was *the one,* and Ron and I had a long marriage, with some stormy spots, as I think most marriages have."

Unexpectedly, the big plane lifted and then abruptly dropped. After levitating, we were slapped down hard in our seats. The seat-belt lights came on and a flight attendant calmed us with the information that incidents like this were not uncommon when flying near the Andes Mountains. She made a joke of it, saying the bump was the prank of a mischievous mountain spirit that occasionally liked to stir things up on an otherwise calm, peaceful flight.

Todd turned to me and teased, "That wasn't the mountain spirit, Jo. You did it! Please don't talk about any more *stormy* spots until we land, OK?"

I grinned, grateful this disturbance hadn't resulted in another whack on my head.

"So what happened," Todd asked, "during that uh... bad time in your marriage?"

"Well, during an extended, difficult period, a tsunami of sorts, he drank every day. I felt so lonely that I resorted to my old addiction of fortifying my self-worth through another man. But, I found this new relationship grew into a gentle love.

"Ironically, just when I had reached the point where I couldn't do it anymore—lead a double life full of guilt—the affair was discovered and ended. But, having grown to love that new man too, losing the relationship was brutal. It felt like a surgical removal, cutting part of my heart away. Do you remember that old song, "Torn between two lovers, feelin' like a fool?"

"Oh yes, I do!"

"Well, it was just like that song. But, I had *always* loved my husband Ron the most—was somehow permanently committed to him, regardless of the unsatisfying situation—and begged him to believe that, to forgive me and take me back. He did, but the devastated look in his eyes set off an irredeemable guilt in me—sin without redemption. The damage I inflicted all around, consumed me.

"We worked through it; he went to counseling and grew into deeper wisdom and compassion, owning some responsibility for the fractured marriage. He eased up on the drinking for a long time—forgave and continued to love me—but I could not love myself any more.

"Guilt is a funny thing. Because I had *sinned*, the pain from that guilt was justified in my mind. It was my penance for the wrongs that I had committed. The more painful, the more I mistakenly thought it 'atoned' or paid for the 'sins'. In my mind, *I deserved all the hell I had created on my earth.*"

Todd's eyes swelled with compassionate tears as he reached out and squeezed my arm.

Answering tears filled my own eyes as I smiled and said, "But Todd, *that's* when the spiritual work of my life began!" I bent forward in the cramped airline seat to stretch my weary back. Todd did the same and when we settled again I said, "Finally, I found *A Course in Miracles,* which is inspired by the teachings of Jesus.

"It saved me."

A Course in Miracles

"One of the first truths I found in *A Course in Miracles* hit me right between the eyes! *'The only thing that could keep me from God's love was GUILT.'* I was effectively blocking out the God who loved me *regardless* of my blunders, sins, errors and failings. I learned that 'sins' are only *errors*—not indelible, irrevocable <u>sin</u>. <u>My</u> God gradually became real, intimate, ever forgiving and unconditionally loving.

"You see, I believe we are punished *by* our 'sins,' not *for* our 'sins.' Holy Spirit uses **all** for good. My sins, or errors, brought me to my knees, opened me up, and in walked miraculous *LOVE.*

"I think we are all born with an 'Achilles Heel,' a gift or challenge that can create hell on earth in our process of working through it. That hell—those *'sins' that never were 'sins,'* **only lessons**—can eventually drive us back to God. It's our free will, our choice to understand—to *grow* from the lessons."

I stopped speaking and realized that the forgiveness lesson I had just experienced last night in Chile, was just a new version of my old, 'favorite sin', guilt. To me, a sin is just something that keeps me away—disconnected from God. My husband's death must have brought it all around again. I guess the lessons will just keep coming until I don't fall for them anymore. Until God's vision of me is the one I accept... a perfect daughter who is learning to love.

Todd and I seemed to be such comfortable companions, so open to each other. "During the period that I studied *A Course in Miracles*, I 'sat' in meditation for an hour before the class. The Presence that came to me sometimes was so unconditionally loving..."

I looked at Todd and wondered if I dared tell him my well-guarded secret vision. He seemed so open, so completely nonjudgmental, and so human (perhaps because he had been the recipient of copious judgment himself).

"Todd, this presence I feel in my meditations and who comes out in my journaling has a sense of humor."

Todd grinned and nodded encouragingly.

I went on, "One night before meditation, I was agonizing over my susceptibility to sexy, intelligent men and beating myself up for it—no actions mind you, just fantasizing. However, I had to acknowledge to myself that the pull was still there.

"During my meditation, a five-second flash of 'vision' came. It was a short, pink, phallic protrusion coming out of the ground like a mushroom. It had funny anemone-like tendrils growing out of it and they were *waving* at me!"

Todd looked confused. "Phallic? You mean...was it a...?" His face blanched as his mouth dropped open.

I nodded "Yes! Well... that pretty well finished off the meditation. I stood up and shook it off a little and tried to analyze what I had just seen.

"Then I *got it* and started to laugh. It was a silly little pink penis, 'popping up again', with extensions that were beckoning to me. Holy Spirit was making fun of my self-flagellations over being so human. This unconditionally loving Presence would not accept my own judgments—even made a joke of them!"

Todd said, "That's *It,* that's the unconditionally loving Voice *I* get!" He grinned and said, "But I sure haven't been privileged to get a vision like yours!

"My gayness, my 'problem', brought me to my knees where I found that powerful, intimate Love. This Presence is sooo personal." He struggled to explain. "I feel like It's so compassionate—almost human—because It seems to understand, on a gut level, the situation we live in on Earth. To live without the awareness of our Oneness, for even a moment—without the love and companionship of the Divine—is devastating."

We sat silently, so grateful for our intimate God-friend. The *Presence* is called by many names, but it is pure *LOVE.*

After ruminating on our conversation for a while, a revelation stunned me. "Todd, I think I've discovered something. Historically, the words sex and spirituality would never have appeared in the same paragraph of writing, let alone in the same sentence. The subjects have been carefully segregated as two things foreign to each other. For centuries the powerful impulse of human sexuality has been denigrated, defamed. Our cultures have considered it a primitive, animalistic impulse and attempted to tightly control it—regulate it."

Todd laughed and said, "Well, it *is* a little like playing with dynamite!"

I nodded my head, laughing too. "It's certainly dangerous. That's probably where it got its bad reputation. But the natural drive of human sexuality is the first step toward romantic love and a mate. You know how everyone agrees that the state of glorious new-found romantic love is an altered reality of consciousness?"

He nodded.

"When we're in that state we see the world through new eyes. *Life is wonderful and our lover is perfect—can do no wrong.* What if that blissful state is really our true consciousness, *not an anomaly,* and it's the closest we humans can get to looking out through the eyes of Divine Love? I think human sexuality opens the door to that Love. We can see it, feel it and experience it. After all, it seems just like the consciousness Sonya described when she passed to the next level of existence in her near-death experience."

I said, "My human wrestlings with sexuality—the very craving I tried to deny and sometimes despised in myself—*started* with my soul yearning for the unconditional love *lost at birth and was then amplified by my father's absence.*" A feeling of relief flooded over me.

I looked at Todd, a little embarrassed to be baring my soul so intimately. I was going out on a long, fragile limb of understanding here.

Comforted, when he nodded back at me with a sweet loving smile of common insight, I continued. "When we are born on Earth, we forget we are part of the Oneness—we forget how precious we are, forget how to love ourselves—so we look for it elsewhere! When we make missteps, stumble and fall in our immature, bumbling attempts at loving, the errors, although painful, are valuable lessons—not reason for condemnation and eternal judgment. These are experiments in learning to love, chances for humans to get a hint, a glimpse of the unfathomable Divine Love.

"Wow!" I slapped my leg in delight and pointed my finger at him. "Our next lesson in unconditional Love extends from the first: we get *children!*

"We look at our new baby, still so full of 'the other side', and we are smitten, consumed with our second dose of unconditional love. We will do <u>anything</u> for that child—throw down our life to save it, if need be..."

After all, what did Jesus do?

The City of Lima

The plane flew on as we leaned over to look out our windows at the jagged Andes mountains. Down there somewhere, the powerful Inca Empire was spawned and, after a brief stop in Lima, we were going to its capitol, Cusco.

In Lima, we found a city of both wealth and horrible poverty. It practically never rains there so it was barren except for irrigated gardens and yards. Some of the wealthy families lived downtown in old Spanish style buildings. The one we visited, covered a full square block bordered by twenty foot walls. The home inside was built around a lush tropical garden courtyard.

Low hills outside the city grew miles of cardboard jungles for the homeless population. After being served with elaborate meals and tucked into a luxurious hotel, our local guide was careful to drive us by the cardboard slums. There were no city sewers and the only water available had to be delivered by a truck. The intended embarrassment spread over us.

Even though the incredible markets of local textiles, jewelry and art were enticing, we realized they were probably created by people paid very little for their work.

A hummingbird pendent of local stones and silver caught Sonya's eye and she bought it. Then she remarked, "I've always loved these little birds. They are so beautiful, but so angry and territorial at the same time. Their wars over my feeders are frightening."

She laughed and told of watching a little female who sat impatiently waiting for the males to quit defending the food without *anyone* getting to eat. She could almost read that little bird's mind— *get over it!* The female bird finally, bravely, decided to go sit on the feeder and drink, disregarding the others. Sonya concluded that the birds mimicked a common pattern of human life as well. "In many places in the world, the choice to fight a war to defend home and family and food results in the very thing the men defend against— the destruction of their home, family and food."

That night we were bussed to an extravagant meal served down in the old town. It was in one of the wealthy homes concealed behind high walls and the huge, rough wood double doors were locked behind us.

Seated at tables scattered throughout the courtyard garden, it felt as if we were in a dense tropical jungle. Two parrots called out throughout the meal. The local guide explained that it was a special privilege to eat here. Silently, I wondered if the family who owned it had fallen on hard times, and were forced to rent their home out to tour groups in order to afford to keep the home intact.

We were invited to a large, colorful seafood buffet. I happened to notice our dark, slender tour member, Takil, as he stopped Todd at the shrimp tray. The man's hand suddenly pressed Todd's down on the table and he said, "The shrimp have gone bad. Don't eat them!" But he didn't take his hand away, causing Todd to look up at him.

The old cliché, "a moment frozen in time," came to mind. I thought the tablecloth might catch on fire from the heat of their eyes and hands. The spell was finally broken when a waiter whisked the offending shrimp tray away.

Hallelujah! Hallelujah! sang out in my mind for them, and I realized that the woman who was traveling with Takil was probably his sister.

As it turned out, there was more drama to be experienced that evening. After dinner the head waiter stood up and announced, "The Governor's home, just around the corner from us, has been the target of an assault. The military has cordoned off six city blocks." Our bus was four blocks away and it would be necessary for us to walk to it in the dark, through unknown conditions.

Nervously collecting our things, we prepared to leave and the waiters volunteered to escort the predominately female group. Jack grabbed two of the silver-haired women and made sure Mildred had a waiter with her. Sonya and I shared our own waiter.

The heavy wood and iron door was opened slightly to peek out and then everyone hurried down the dark streets. Ironically, our waiter "accidentally" took the opportunity to pass his hand across my breast as he was "protecting" me. Since we were practically running, I gave him the benefit of the doubt.

Breathless, back on the bus, and realizing that the danger was behind us—we all agreed that this would be one more adventure to tell back at home. Jack's two older ladies and Mildred remarked that they hadn't had that much excitement in twenty years.

---

13   Yearning for Cusco

Sonya woke us early the next morning so we could be ready for traveling the short flight to Cusco. When we arrived at the airport, we learned that the plane was three hours delayed, the toilets were stopped up and there were crowds of people listlessly milling around. It was interesting to see a cross section of Lima's population (the ones who could afford to fly). From nuns in their black habits to young people and families in western attire, we were all in the same situation, stuck on the ground of the airport.

As I looked around at the people, I noticed an elderly man watching our trio of silver-haired ladies. He seemed to be summoning up his courage to approach them. Finally, he hitched up his belt with a showy silver buckle, in a vain attempt to pull his pants up over his protruding belly, and approached them.

"Hello you lovely ladies," he said. "I'm from the South and I heard your Southern drawls; I'm lonesome for Americans. What are you good women doin' so far from home?"

Mildred straightened her shoulders and perked up. I watched in amusement as she became animated… coquettish. "We're with this tour group traveling around South America." She proudly gestured out to our multi-cultural troupe. "We've got Jews, Muslims and Hindu people with us."

He looked perplexed. Bending down close to her he asked, "Why would you want to travel with those people? Hell, they don't even believe in *God*. And Jews are the Christ killers!" He straightened up, swelled out his chest and firmly announced, "You should be around God fearin' *Christian* folks. Those people are different from us. Ya know, they *are* goin' to hell 'cause they don't believe in *Jesus!*"

He wore his prejudice like a badge of honor. It served as a raincoat wrapped around his body as if to prevent even one drop of truth from touching him, threatening to dilute his hard shell of righteousness.

Mildred looked back at him and I saw mixed emotions flit across her face. She said, "Well, I know what we've been taught, that only through Jesus are they saved from hell."

He interrupted, "Damn right! Their heathen ways could rub off on you pretty ladies."

She stared back at him. Hesitantly, in a small voice, she replied, "Well, I guess they have rubbed off a little. I've been visiting with each one of them, trying to spread the 'good news of Jesus', but every one of them already worships God, just in a different way. And the Muslims pray five times a day! Every time I look at 'em, *they're praying again*. I don't think God will turn his back on all that prayer—on those people." Her two friends chimed in, agreeing with her.

The old man stood up abruptly and turned to leave. Over his shoulder, he spat out, "You women had better git on *your* knees and pray ten times a day to get your good sense back!"

As he stalked past me, I ducked my head to hide the smile on my face. The act of bonding together into a shared prejudice against "the other," *can* be a good ice breaker, a way into a new conversation or relationship, but this time it had back-fired on the old boy.

I turned to notice Sonya wiggling and fretting in her airport seat. "I've studied the *National Geographic* photos of Machu Picchu till they're worn out," she complained. "I want to see the real thing!"

Jack came around and informed everyone it would be a long wait because our plane was being repaired and was still in Cusco. He then grabbed an empty chair next to me to visit with us. My senses went on alert, aware of his warmth and the scent of him.

"Tell us a little about your Hindu religion Sonya," I prompted, partially to calm her impatience and to distract myself.

Sonya looked at me and the group and accepted the invitation.

Sonya's Explanation of Hinduism

"We Hindu's believe our world is a multiple-layered world that includes innumerable galaxies horizontally, innumerable tiers vertically, and innumerable cycles temporally."

"Wait a minute!" I leaned forward in my seat opposite her. "I need to understand what you just said. I get that earth is amongst uncountable galaxies, but what is this tier business, vertically?"

"We believe that as we progress up the spiritual ladder of 'enlightenment' we will experience many levels of existence beyond this one Earth school. But we have to 'get it right' here on earth in multiple lives first. That's the innumerable temporal cycles.

"We believe this is a moral world where the law of 'karma'—what goes around comes around—is never suspended. So to get off this merry-go-round of Earth, we have to live *right* and pay back *wrong* actions before we can go on to the next level."

Rachael interjected, "Are you suggesting that my daughter has to go through being abused and beaten up because she might have been the bully herself, the last time around?"

Shrugging her tiny sari-covered shoulders, Sonya smiled at her and said, "Could be. Or maybe it's the next time around that she gets to knock *him* senseless when he comes back as a woman!" Everyone laughed, thoroughly enjoying the theoretical retribution.

Sonya continued, "Earth is only a middle world that will never replace paradise as the spirit's destination. It's a world that is *maya*, deceptively tricky in posing as the <u>ultimate</u> reality, with its many varied experiences, beautiful gifts, and the play of good versus evil when these things are actually <u>temporary</u>. It's a training ground on which people can develop their highest capacities."

"Kind'a like boot camp in the marines, huh?" asked Jack. He then jumped up and did some pretty fine "jumping jack" exercises to amuse his impatient troupe.

Sonya laughed with the rest of us at his addition to the conversation. "No... I sometimes think it's the actual *war* itself. So difficult and so compelling at the same time."

She pointed out that the Hindus believe that Earth life is usually composed of three stages—the first stage being the student. The second stage begins, ideally, with love and marriage and the interests of family, vocation and community. There are joys and challenges to be encountered. The strong pull of the male/female sexuality can be misunderstood, misused and abused at the expense of other people and pursued as the most important aspect of life.

She said, "Some of us believe that a soul enthralled with sexuality *should* pursue, search out, and experience all that sex has to offer—all those aspects, hopefully with moral consideration—*but to continue to do it until that soul realizes that sex is not the ultimate goal. Only then, through <u>intense</u> <u>experience</u>, can the tight grip of physical obsession be loosened—allowing the soul to explore and experience sex from a more balanced perspective.*"

Todd was happily sitting with Takil, but raised his eyes to meet mine when we heard Sonya's last words.

Sonya went on, "Also power, wealth, prestige and material toys can be pursued in search of ultimate happiness until *they too*, lose their value. There is nothing like experience to get the point across. Human life is change, constant change, from birth until death's transition. Life is all about bringing up enthralling elements that need to be experienced and explored—then the obsession is worn out and discarded. That is where true freedom is attained."

We were amazed. She offered no sense of judgment, no "threat of hell" for giving in to the urge to explore it all—to taste everything in life before it is over.

Jack rose up and his arms encircled the women as if he were herding them. With a lecherous grin directed at Sonya he said, "You're telling me that I should continue to chase and enjoy all you lovely women and scramble to attain notoriety and the power it brings, as long as I want to?"

Laughter erupted from the group.

Sonya looked at him with the sweetest, loving smile and twinkling eyes and said, "Yes Jack. You will not be satisfied and happy or gain internal wisdom about it all unless you experience it for yourself. Religious laws are in place to guide us on a painless path, a fruitful path. But we reeeealy have to live it to actually *know*. Treat them gently, Rooster Jack. Just remember—you will eventually get to play the part of all those pursued and discarded women."

While enjoying the group's laughter, he glanced at me with a penetrating look that seemed to say, "I'm feeling discarded already, thanks to you."

"The third and last stage of life is the most important," Sonya concluded, "To find *meaning* in the mystery of existence—this is life's final and most daunting challenge.

"We ultimately believe that this is a world of *Lila*, the play of the Divine in its Cosmic Dance."

Our group sat back in silence and mulled over the new information of Sonya's spiritual beliefs, comparing it with our own.

Takil said, "This seems to be a new-age slant to the whole spiritual subject, presented by one of the oldest religions. I wonder if there really is new knowledge to be found or is it only a 'remembering'?"

Once again, Sonya spoke. "We Hindus have lived among all different religions for centuries. From experience, we feel that the various spiritualities are but different languages through which God speaks to the human heart."

"Yes," Medina agreed. "The Koran says that Allah sent messengers to all peoples so that they could know God."

Sonya finished her information with an old Hindu story.

"It is possible to climb life's mountain from any side, but when the top is reached, ***the trails converge***. Differences in culture, history, geography, and collective temperament all make for beautifully diverse starting points. It adds richness to the total human venture! Is life not more interesting for the many varied contributions? Taoists, Buddhists, Muslims, Jews, Christians...?

"So, the lesson of the story! While all these people are climbing to the top, if someone is going around the bottom and trying to get them all to climb *his* path, '*the only right, true path*,' that someone is not diligently climbing up his *own* path."

CHRISTIANITY AND BUDDHISM *"Western man has been turning outwards toward the world of the senses for centuries and losing himself in outer space. He has to learn again to turn inwards and find his Self. He has to learn to explore not outer space but inner space within the heart, to make that long and difficult journey to the Centre, to the inner depth and height of Being which Dante described in the 'Divine Comedy," compared with which the exploration of the moon and other planets is the play of children."*

Bede Griffiths - English Benedictine Monk
1906—1993, Missionary to India for 50 years

---

14 Jack

No wonder Jo is hanging around Sonya so much. Jack felt himself drawn into her illusive circle of lovingness like the rest of them.

What a different and refreshing take on life she embodied! Guessing that this exploration of spirituality wasn't their first, he wanted to be included in the future discussions. Maybe that's why they disappeared so often—to hole up and talk.

He had been feeling a subtle rejection from Jo. Well, it wasn't actually rejection because she often looked at him with open fondness. She just wasn't available.

In fact she was downright elusive. He chuckled at the irony of *his* getting to experience what a *woman* went through as she became another notch on some man's gun. He felt like something delicious that Jo had tasted on an abundant buffet, and then she went on in search of dessert.

Oh No! It was already happening to him—*karma!*

Like an adolescent, he stubbornly tried to show he didn't care. The rooster dance in Santiago had been beefed up partially for her. But that *did* get a little out of control. He flushed a bit at the memory.

The tour was rolling on, more countries behind them than ahead. He urgently wanted to be with Jo, to get to explore her— mind *and* body. But performing the many hidden duties of a tour guide left little time to do anything about it. Always the airline tickets were to be handed out at each airport and the luggage to be checked, trundled to the plane and then delivered upon arrival, to the appropriate rooms. Then the accommodations might be screwed up—unhappy people to be appeased. Someone always got sick and needed a doctor. Throughout the whole tour, unavoidable challenges kept him hopping.

With a small group like this, there wasn't any extra money for a second person to help him with all the details, but it was worth it. His reward was getting to guide folks through foreign discoveries, and then to lecture on subjects that fascinated him. It was always compelling and ever-changing.

Cusco and Machu Picchu never failed to entrance and he looked forward to sharing these sites with first timers, but this trip was turning out to be a special one. He remembered his initial fear at the airport, of being presented with a bunch of "religious people" who were dull and way too serious, unable to loosen up and play. He had to laugh at himself. Man—had he been wrong. Most of these folks were enthusiastic, curious and game for *anything!*

Now, if that damned plane would just get fixed and make the short hop down the mountain to them after its three hour delay, they could leave the swirling Peruvian masses and clogged toilets behind. He longed to inhale that crisp cold mountain air of Cusco.

He wove his way through the bedraggled, long-suffering group and approached Sonya with a request. "Could I sit with you on our plane trip uphill to Cusco? I'm intrigued by your Hindu belief system."

"Of course, Jack! I'd love to visit with you," she answered.

Back-dropped by blue mountains, their plane finally arrived. It taxied onto the runway outside the two-story airport terminal windows and the luggage was loaded. Jack started counting heads as they boarded, only to find his trio of gray-haired ladies missing again. He sent Medina to check in the restrooms, where she found them frantically making their last minute pit stop in the very smelly facilities.

At last! They felt the plane lift off and turn to head for the mountains in the distance. Sonya peered greedily out the little window for a while and then focused her expectant smile on him.

"So Jack! What *shall* we talk about?"

"I want to make sure I heard you correctly about your Hindu second phase of life. You *did* say it was advisable to pursue whatever consumes us in that stage, right?"

She grinned mischievously, "Absolutely. That's what we're here for—to experience and live whatever pulls at us. That urge is telling you what you need to explore, to learn about in this life. Nothing is ultimately good or bad. It all fits together to complete our evolution."

He stared at her, hesitantly admitting, "Monogamy is pretty difficult for me."

Her eyes dancing, she replied, "It's a more peaceful road to travel, that monogamy, and marketed strenuously by our religions so we can experience less pain, more peace, and hopefully not build up bad karma.

"Cultures have had very different standards for regulating sexual expression since human time began. The Eskimos shared their women with weary travelers. Many cultures accepted, even *expected* the powerful men to keep concubines. The Bible says that Abraham took a second wife in order to produce a son, which culminated in the religion of Islam.

"Look at the diversity in the animal kingdom. Swans and penguins mate for life. Wolves choose permanent mates if possible, but are not adverse to 'a little on the side'. Dominant male gorillas take on the responsibility of guarding a whole band of animals, but also take mating rights with all the females they wish.

"The males of some species, like elk, only pass through at rutting season, where the strongest wins the contested female for survival of the species." She laughed and added, "The black widow male spider chases the much larger succulent female and after he 'has his way with her', *she eats him!*"

Jack flinched, "Aw, c'mon... Really?"

Smiling, Sonya continued, "I think humans come in with different mating impulses for a reason—lessons. The monogamous ones can have a peaceful life while the others may have lives full of exciting and often painful educational adventures.

"I read a story about a righteous man who craved to 'dally' outside his marriage, but would *not* because it was a *sin*. When he died he very proudly acknowledged his abstention and the advisors on the other side said, *"*You were *supposed to dally!* How will you actually know for yourself that it's ultimately unsatisfying? You are still longing for it." So they gave him a dimension in Heaven to indulge to his heart's content—to learn for himself—that boundary-less sex *wasn't* the satisfying and fulfilling experience he imagined it would be—no matter how many partners or times he had it!"

Jack shook his head in disbelief, "You are a very unusual woman, Sonya. So… while I'm confessing, it needs to be said that I don't care much for formal religion either. I have awe and intense curiosity about what makes up our reality—the information coming from *everywhere* to help us fill in the puzzle pieces—but religion… not so much."

Sonya laughed out loud, "Me too! All that fuss with creeds, rules, regulations, judgments and boxes we try to lock God into. We attempted to create God in our own image, to understand Him better, and we *did*. But our Creator, our Source—Love Itself—is not to be tamed with our human laws, no matter how well intended and cherished. Isn't that wonderful?

"Our religions do give us valuable paths to God, but I also think we can find God through chasing our 'bliss.' You are doing that, in part, with your exciting vocation, the thing that enthralls you and crowds out anything else.

"But Jack, that glorious mind and intellect of yours can only get you so far. The way to contact and experience your Source within is through noticing and feeling those emotions of appreciation and love that come up, not just for special people, but for others along the way, like our precious silver-haired ladies that have warmed your heart.

"It shows, Jack! You are loving them just as they are, flawed and eccentric. That's how your Divine nature comes out into the world—your joyous, playful, even 'wicked' Divine nature!"

Jack impulsively grabbed her two little hands and brought them to his lips and kissed them. Looking deep into her eyes he said, "I wish you were *younger*, precious woman—I would quite thoroughly love you—*and then leave you!*"

Not to be outdone, Sonya laughed, "And I would love *you*, you devilish rogue, so *thoroughly* that you'd stay way longer than you intended!"

They doubled over in belly-laughs so loud that the other passengers turned around, trying to see what they might be missing.

CHRISTIANITY *"Oh God, You have declared me perfect in your eyes. You have always cared for me in my distress; now hear me as I call again. Have Mercy upon me. Hear my prayer."*

Psalms 7:4

---

15 Cusco

Finally, up in the air again, we glimpsed the mighty Andes and then landed after a short flight. Cusco is a beautiful old stone city nestled in a high lush valley, at eleven thousand feet. Having just been at sea level, it took our breath away!

Tucked into a nice hotel, we were served *coca leaf tea* and encouraged to nap. Jack said that the tea and a nap is the local remedy for altitude shock. I had heard about the coca leaves that were meted out, in ancient times, for Inca workers to chew for strength and a feeling of well-being. Those hardy little men, who built the retaining walls and carried soil from the lowlands and bat guano from the caves, made it possible to grow crops from the Inca days until now—quite a feat!

Medina asked, "Is this cocaine? Will we get 'high'?"

"Yes! You most certainly will get and *are* very high right now," snorted Rachael.

Sonya peered into the warm inviting cup and then took the first sip. I tried mine. It was pale yellow and I found it to be bland—not remarkable—but nice. No one noticed much affect, but went on to bed for a little nap as instructed. We found out later that coca leaves are the raw product used to make cocaine, but the concentration in the tea is very small compared to actual cocaine, simply a medicinal dose.

Donning light coats because it was cooler at this elevation, Sonya, Rachael and I collected Todd and Takil to stroll through the narrow streets of stone with the rest of the tour group. The Inca buildings had been torn down to erect new Spanish homes, but fortunately, there were still some ancient Incan walls to be admired.

Jack circulated through the clusters of our tour group and explained, "The polished stones are massive and irregularly shaped but still somehow fit together so exactly that a pocket knife blade won't fit between them. Built without mortar, these walls have withstood generations of earthquakes because the way they were laid enables them to move slightly, but then settle back into place. The Incas had no wheels, no steel, and no pack horses, only little llamas." Again, he made a strong case for the likelihood of extraterrestrial assistance in the building of these amazing Incan structures.

I thought back to my own gardens and my painstakingly built, dry-stacked rock walls. They always moved and deteriorated after very little time unless I used mortar, and mortar only slowed down the process a little while. Man! What a miracle we were seeing.

Cathedral bells chimed the time and we had to head back to the hotel. Spicy smells of food drifted out from closed doors in the impenetrable walls of the private homes along the way. Our stomachs growled in longing.

"Wait!" called Todd, and he and Takil scooped up some beautiful watercolors of the cobbled streets where we had walked, painted by a tiny, toothless woman. When her daughters came around the corner carrying their baby sister, they realized she was a young mother and paid a bit more for her art work. The high altitude, dry air, strong sun, and hard life seemed to weather everyone's skin even though the adults all wore sturdy little black hats.

That night Jack mesmerized us with pictures of Nazca, a 50 mile long, high desert plain in southern Peru. He said, "There are hundreds of gigantic drawings up there, stretched out across the plain. They were created between 400 and 650 AD by removing the rampant reddish pebbles to expose a white lime base. These works of art included figures of hummingbirds, monkeys, spiders, fish, sharks, orcas, llamas and lizards and also, trees and flowers. I can't actually *show* you the sight unless we rent a plane and fly over—all of this is only recognizable from the air!"

"And these drawings have been there since around 400 AD?" Todd looked at Jack with a puzzled expression.

"That's right," answered Jack.

"I don't understand how the native population could possibly create such accurate pictures, from the ground." He wrestled with the concept. "It's as if they were drawing a representation of the life on earth for someone, some beings up in the sky! They must have had some contact with aliens to go to such trouble."

Jack then showed us photos of geometric shapes and the most amazingly straight architectural lines crossing each other, covering miles. We saw a recent satellite photo and it truly looked like an engineer had drawn the straight intersecting lines. He said, "One theory of Swiss author, Erich von Daniken, is that it was a landing runway for extra-terrestrials."

Well, old Jack was still stirring our minds with his knowledge. He told of recent "sightings," here in Peru—moving lights up in the night skies that sometimes worked in groups and made formations, only to instantly shoot off away from each other and disappear. These could be seen all over the world but were very frequent in Peru.

We made a conscious effort to check the skies for the rest of our trip.

The next morning we were bussed to the fortress of *Sacsayhauaman* *or Saksaqwaman,* perched on the hills overlooking Cusco in its lush green valley. However you spell the name, it sounds like "saxywoman," and Jack relished this oddity by gutturally rolling the name off his tongue with a mischievous grin.

The massive limestone blocks of this site were among the largest of all the Incan ruins. Again, even though the edges were rounded, a piece of paper wouldn't fit between them. The fortress overlooked a large plaza capable of holding thousands and was probably used for ceremonies.

Today, the current inhabitants of the area could be seen wading through the thick green grass. They were brightly costumed native women and children who led small llamas that sported colorful tassels from the tips of their long ears.

Everyone was encouraged to take pictures, for a fee. My urge to pet a llama was strong—those big, soft eyes and dense, curly fur—but I remembered that the animals don't like to be touched. They stood, aloof and stoic, patiently waiting for their human companions to do what humans do.

For a while, I stood away from the crowd and breathed in the crisp air, air scented with the crushed grass beneath our feet. "Crisp" was an inadequate adjective for that miraculous air—the clean, humidity-free, absolutely clear, fresh atmosphere stretching to a sky so intensely blue that it almost hurt my eyes.

There were flutes for sale, and my favorite, the pan flute, was being demonstrated. The pan flute is a combination of several hollow tubes woven together, in a line, by brightly colored yarn. A practiced musician was creating breathy haunting notes that echoed across that mountain air. I bought a recording of the song *Flight of the Condor,* played with those flutes. The special song of the Andes, it celebrates the condors, huge buzzard-like birds with seven-foot wing spans that majestically sail high on the wind currents of the mountains.

Todd was as entranced with the flutes as I was and enthusiastically bought one of the pan flutes. Then he tried to play it! More difficult than he imagined, he doggedly struggled to make a pleasant combination of sounds come out of the slender pipes. Takil put his hand out to pat his friend's shoulder in sympathetic support and left it there a moment too long. As I turned away I caught a glimpse of Mildred, ever alert for evidence of *sin*, whispering to her friends and pointing. She frowned at the couple and pursed her lips in disapproval.

Next, the bus took us to the infamous train that follows the Urubamba River up to Machu Picchu. That train ride was an adventure in itself! It stopped at numerous little communities and people got off and on. One platform held a woman bent over a large pot full of fragrant corn tamales that she was selling. The aroma made our mouths water, but we had been warned not to buy *anything* out of the train window so we resisted, picturing a possible gastrointestinal event later.

But when one of the stops revealed the most beautiful wool, hand-loomed blanket, I caved in. It was of a pattern I had not seen in all the displays in Lima or Cusco and held up by the woman who had painstakingly *made it.* I scrambled with my Peruvian money. Not having enough, I went to American dollars and, still not having enough, went to my appalled companions. They generously dug deep even though they appeared disturbed by my impulsive purchase. The woman threw the blanket into the train window after the last money was thrown out. She looked confused as the train swiftly pulled away, and I hoped that I had paid her enough.

Suddenly, I was alone on my bench seat. Even Sonya moved far away. My scattered companions were heeding the warning of louse-infected blankets that could be sold, just as I had bought mine. I was a little nervous, but not too much. Everyone else was alarmed and no one sat with me for the entire trip until I managed to get double plastic bags to entomb the imagined little critters (which, happily, never appeared).

On and on up the mountain we rode on two tiny rails perched precariously above the Urubumba river that raged furiously down in the ravine below. Beside us on the steep slope were beautiful stone terraces built by generations of coca leaf chewing Incas, and maintained well to this day for raising crops.

We reached the end of the train line and transferred to yet another bus. The tail end of the trip proved to be three huge switchbacks of road that allowed the straining bus to traverse the steep incline.

As we got on the bus, two ragged little boys, maybe ten years old, smiled broadly and waved at us to get our attention. Abruptly, they then plunged into the upper jungle, just as the bus pulled away from the train. Upon making it around the first switch-back and on the straight road, the two boys burst out of the lower jungle, waved and laughed, and as we watched with amazed amusement, plunged into the upper jungle. They were racing the bus to the top! The scene repeated itself on the second straight-away and finally at the top the two waited in the road, waving wildly and laughing. Of course everyone took their pictures and gave them money for such a monumental feat. I wondered how many times they would repeat their act for the nearly 2,000 people who visit daily.

Machu Picchu

A beautiful garden with orchids and tropical plants that I didn't recognize greeted us at the final bus stop. My temptation to examine them more closely was quickly thwarted when my gaze lifted to the slope above which held a miracle of mysterious stone constructions shrouded in blankets of clouds. The experienced local guide was a slim, beautiful woman with straight shining black hair cut in a long bob that flipped as she led us up and down the terraces of the now familiar smooth, carefully placed rocks. A misty cloud swirled around our heads, felt cool against our cheeks, and eventually built up little crystals on the tips of our eyelashes.

We were shown the stone trough remains of a water system that had supplied the whole complex—enough water from two springs to irrigate the crops grown on terraces for the inhabitants. A few of the small stone houses had been restored with little thatch roofs to give an idea of the original dwellings.

Our enthusiastic guide gathered us into a group in front of one of the little houses and began to explain the history of this magic mountain ruin. "A 14th century wonder of the world, Machu Picchu is situated eight thousand feet above sea level on a mountain ridge nestled in with other sacred mountains of the Inca—and of the civilization that preceded them. A legal document was found from 1568, forty years after the Spanish Conquest of Peru, stating that the Inca Ruler, Patchacutec, built Machu Picchu. Miraculously, the Spanish never found and looted it, as they had done with many other sites." The guide's shoulders straightened with pride as she suggested that Picchu's original builders had carefully selected the hidden, remote site with security in mind.

"After Picchu was 'lost' for 400 years," she continued, "Hiram Bingham III, a Yale professor, found it again in 1911. He had the help of an eleven year old boy—the son of two farmers who had moved higher up the valley to avoid taxation. Nearly consumed by the jungle, the ruins required extensive work to reveal their magnitude. Hiram took all of the discovered artifacts back to Yale and they were recently returned to us thanks to a protest by the Peruvian government. When studied, these artifacts revealed that the ruler had enjoyed such luxuries as a private stone bath, meals served on silver plates, and relaxation in an orchid-scented garden."

In this awe-inspiring, majestic setting, my only regret of the day was that I could not find a way to be still and absorb the feeling—the sense of the place—while it was filled with noisy people as delighted as I was.

Finally, an opportunity presented itself when a serious drizzle started to fall and there was a generalized scurrying for cover. Ignoring the fact that I was getting drenched, I persisted and stood alone at the "Temple of the Sun" and gazed out at the mountains protecting our terraced ruin. Those mountains that rose *straight up* to the heavens like giant green cones with rounded tops, would forever hold the secrets of the people who had once lived here. I wondered about their concept of God.

Someone appeared at my side, brushed against my arm and I was pleased to find Jack, standing in the rain also. He said, "I always feel *awe*, no matter how many times I come here." He leaned into me and our shoulders touched as we stood in reverent silence. Finally, soggy but satisfied, we went down to the group to meet the bus.

No bus!

The local guide called for information and was told that a small landslide had occurred half-way up our hill on the road below us and had to be cleared so the bus could get through.

Rachael joked, "It was probably started by our ten-year-old mountain-climbing boys."

We were informed that the bus probably wouldn't be back for at least an hour.

Jack said, "Well… that translates to two or three hours."

The rain had stopped and, even with wet fannies, it was pleasant sitting on the steps to wait. Flowers perfumed the air that brushed across our faces. Sonya noted, "We could be stuck in worse places."

The Climb

The guide fastened her dark eyes on a neighboring mountain and suggested a short trek up to watch for the return of a hiking party that was to arrive at the hotel. The group had walked four days on the Inca Trail – locally also known as the Trail to the Sun.

Describing both the ancient rock gate to Picchu that they would pass under and also the spectacular view, she said it would be fun for the brave of heart. The trail was narrow and steep, but short.

Flushed with the surreal atmosphere of the day and probably Jack's presence, I volunteered to go.

"No… No thank you," echoed through the rest of our intimate party. Two or three younger folks and Jack and I gathered around her, eager for one more thrill.

About twenty minutes into the hike I wondered, *what the hell was I thinking?* Only three feet wide, the path was restricted on the one side by vertical cliffs and the other edge, straight down to sure death.

"We're almost there," encouraged the guide, "Senora, just two ladders to the top."

Two ladders? I looked up to see Tarzan vines—thick, shaggy vines fashioned into ladders that stretched up the face of the cliff. ... "Who *knows* how old these dilapidated vines are," I muttered under my breath.

Embarrassed to fail in front of Jack, I valiantly attacked the first of the two "ladders". As my hands clenched the vines, chips of bark peeled off and stuck to my sweaty palms. *How many chips till there's no ladder*, I wondered. Doggedly climbing to its top, and breathing heavily in the thin air, I turned around, looked down, and *froze!*

"Oh my God! My God!" I whimpered. Still on the narrow trail far below, Jack's face looked up at me, watching. That didn't help. I shook with fright. The ledge I was standing on seemed two feet wide and emptied straight down to the bottom of the world.

I side-stepped to the next ladder and clamped a sweating hand on it. *That* hand in a death grip, I swung my other arm around in front of my face, grabbed the ladder and turned into the mountain, so I wasn't looking down. *That was it! I wasn't moving! Up or down.*

With eyes squeezed shut I made an effort to take in deep breaths. Fearfully, I opened my eyes to face the sheer wall and focused on the rock face. Grey-green lichen decorated the surface. Those tiny creations take years to creep two inches across the rocks. These specimens were six inches wide and had been staring down our mountainous valley for generations. They belonged here. *I didn't!*

The rest of our tiny climbing group, except for Jack, were at the top already, talking with excited voices. The Inca Trail hiking party had arrived. A brown Sherpa face popped over the cliff to peer at me from the top. I looked up at him with wild, white-rimmed eyes. He knew that look.

That sturdy fellow, whose shoulders were almost as wide as he was tall, had toted all the party's equipment for four days! But he swung out over the cliff and easily—like a monkey—jumped down the ladder to me. The ladder shook with his descent and I panicked all over again.

Balancing on the narrow ledge with ease, he soothed me.

"Missy, you okay! You okay!" Putting his hand on my shoulder he said, "I get you down. Is okay, Missy."

"I'm not moving!" I said. I put my head down and wouldn't look at him.

A stubby arm reached back into his pack and pulled out leaves. *Leaves!* He put one under my resistant nose. "You chew Missy, you chew."

Coca leaves, my mind registered. Coca leaves. I shook my head, no! I needed all my faculties to deal with this emergency.

He coaxed one into my clenched hand. "You feel stronger. You feel better."

Reluctantly, letting go of the ladder with that hand, I put one in my dry mouth and grabbed back on. There was no saliva to soften it. I chewed anyway. A sharp taste caused my mouth to fill with moisture and I chewed with more success.

"More, you chew *more* now..." He handed me a second leaf.

I did. After a little bit I noticed my grip on the ladder wasn't so frantic. The rapid breathing was gone.

I looked at him. "That's good stuff!" I said.

He grinned, showing brown teeth. "You OK now Missy, you good, now."

I was! He held my back as I steadily climbed my way to the top. I was greeted by a gorgeous scarlet sunset—framed by the rock gate at the top of the world.

Grateful tears of relief poured down my cheeks and I grabbed that little man and hugged him till he protested, "OK! OK now."

Laughing in the middle of my tears, I thought, *Thank God for ancient herbal remedies!*

The traveling party went on down, eager to get to the hotel and baths.

The Sherpa held back and coached me down, "No look down, Missy. Look at ladder and mountain. No look down." It was easy from then on.

The bus was another hour coming but I didn't care. Sitting on the steps next to Jack, who had witnessed the whole thing, I told of the adventure. Jack added, "Those coca leaves are valuable up here. They give you a feeling of well-being and strengthen your heart. It helps with the thin air, the altitude."

My friends wanted to know what it felt like after chewing the coca leaves. I started to jump up, "I'll go find the Sherpa—get you some."

"No, No, just rest there," they laughed, and pushed me back down.

The bus finally came. Back down the hill… bus, then train, and then bus delivered us to Cusco again. A short plane ride in the dark dropped us back down into Lima and a very welcome hotel.

Sonya and I were exhausted. Extreme changes of altitude, excitement and the energy-sapping exploration of Machu Picchu had finally drained the last strength from our drooping bodies. We holed up in the room and ordered room service of spaghetti and salad.

My last thought, before sleep over-took me, was to realize *God had answered my frantic call from the mountains with an unlikely solution—a Sherpa with drugs!*

Guayaquil

Next morning, very early, the troupe boarded the plane for Ecuador and landed in the sea-level city of Guayaquil. An impression of claustrophobic heat, humidity and a plague of mosquitoes is all I can remember.

As I smashed a sucking, swelling mosquito, I was grateful for my required yellow fever inoculation, administered at home before the trip.

We craved to get on that next plane to the highlands of Quito, but we had to wait, yet again. Our impression of Guayaquil may have been colored by the fact that Sonya and I were becoming very ill.

HINDUISM *"Howsoever men try to worship Me, I welcome them. By whatever path they travel, it leads to Me at last."*

The Bhagavad Gita, Chapter 4

---

16   Quito Ecuador

I spent a lot of the short flight up to the highlands of Quito in the cramped airplane bathroom. Sonya wondered what was wrong until the stomach cramps hit her while she was on the hotel elevator, after we finally arrived at our destination. Appalled, she found herself assaulted with uncontrollable diarrhea as we scurried down the long hall to our room and bathroom.

A short time later, I felt sturdy enough to peep out into the hall to investigate voices and noises of bumping and scraping that had persisted for a while. A slightly crippled janitor was on his hands and knees, cleaning the carpets, with his manager standing over him. The soiled trail on the carpet led straight to our door.

Totally embarrassed, I apologized profusely for the mess. The manager translated my message to the janitor and he quietly responded. The manager then interpreted his words. "These things happen to Americans here in our country. If it attacks you again Senora, would you just *please stand still?"*

Jack had called the hotel physician, after realizing our distress, and notified us that the doctor was coming. But, Jack wouldn't dare come to check on us himself.

A short, friendly physician arrived and proceeded to try to chat a lot while examining our situation. We weren't chatting. Alternating between chills and fever under five blankets and emergency trips to the bathroom, we choreographed and performed a strange duet-dance. Once I missed a step and had to lose my breakfast in the waste basket.

The doctor sat in the one chair and watched us "dance", like one would watch a ping-pong match, waiting for an opening. Finally, he just started talking to the one in the bed.

He decided that we had the usual bug for Americans, tourista squirtus maximus. I blamed the Lima room service spaghetti.

He said that a shot of Demerol and Phenergan would help. "Trouble is, I only have one injection with me." Of course the elder Sonya with her thin little body needed it the most, so I toughed it out without much help.

Twenty-four hours later we emerged from our room, trembling and empty, afraid to try anything to eat. Sonya said, "Tomorrow, when we pack, I think the commode should go with us. We have become very attached to it."

Our lost twenty-four hours was the day tour of Quito and *all* of its cathedrals. We didn't mind having missed that; the tour had already been sufficiently full of cathedrals.

Today was to be a trip to a native farmer's market out into the absolutely gorgeous mountains. The crisp temperature and clear air helped to revive us, and when the bus stopped at a wayside park, where a woman was selling corn tamales in the shucks, we sampled the food. Jack knew this woman and always stopped to eat there. It was just a mixture of fresh corn and cornmeal but it seemed like ambrosia—just the right thing for tender tummies.

The market was in a distant village, but it was worth it. Many, many tiny brown native people were shopping, laughing and chattering. The women were all dressed gaily in multi-colored shawls and full, gathered skirts. The men wore dark colored shirts and slacks. All sported the same little black short-brimmed hats of the Peruvians.

There were gunny-sacks rolled open on the ground with incredibly aromatic fresh herbs of all descriptions, some of them purported to cure infertility, or to catch a husband, or to increase desire in the bedroom. Pots of all kinds of food simmered away, and hot oil fried up the small local fish that people ate with their fingers.

We saw a little woman with three children swarming around her, and with another one on her back supported by her shawl. She fed them bits of a whole fish, somehow eliminating the bones.

The most amazing thing about the open-air market was five, foot-operated sewing machines busily humming away, run by five *men*. The machines sat on wide concrete steps that overlooked the busy shopping area in the field below. The used clothing being purchased, could be altered *on the spot.*

For the first time, I detected a feebleness in Sonya. The illness had hit her hard and she needed to rest often. We climbed back on the bus early and were in the front seats as the others came back aboard.

After all were reloaded, an attractive young native man, with the shiniest thick brown braid of hair down his back, came in with a rack of little rosy-colored bananas for sale. Everyone bought and sampled their delicious sweetness. Sonya and I, seemingly recovered from our illness, greedily devoured two apiece.

The supper meal was scheduled early so that the mossy brick restaurant located fairly close to the market could be enjoyed. It was delightfully enveloped in pendulous trees and sweeping vines. After a hearty meal, there was plenty of time to linger over excellent coffee, so everyone leaned back in comfortable chairs around the table and chatted about the native market and Ecuador in general. I thought that this little country was my favorite of the whole trip, possibly because I was just back from a close encounter with hell.

The discussion at our table eventually turned to spirituality and became so animated that it attracted several more tour people and Jack, who pulled up closer in order to hear better. I was slightly alarmed to see Mildred and her side-kicks pull up chairs on the periphery of the group. At an early point during the discussion, she stood up abruptly and stalked to the bathroom, but she did return to sit and listen.

The Separation

The story of Adam and Eve came up and Rachael said, "My thoughts are that in eating 'from the tree of knowledge', Adam and Eve's perception changed—life in the Garden of Eden was seen through eyes that began to look for good *and evil*. Before that, it was all *good*. They saw their nakedness and called it evil. God became someone to be feared, and they hid. The separation began. That was the beginning of the *insanity*. We broke up the *perfect* concept of Creation into good or bad, and struck out into the wilderness, to wander alone, without God."

"That *is* Insanity!" Sonya interjected. "Humans cannot leave God—our Source, the Love that is our animating force. *Life itself* is God in disguise. We can't tear our sacred hearts out and still walk this earth."

Sonya went on, "At everyone's core is an Unconditional Love so great that *nothing* could cause it to turn away from us. The Beloved is right where we are, accepting us just as we are—that Love cherishes us, wants nothing more than to dance with us—we whom the Beloved has created.

"But we think we're alone—fragile, vulnerable, indelibly flawed—we think we have to scratch and claw our way to the top of the mountain all by ourselves. The concept of the *personal self* arrives right on schedule in our children at two years old. There is an abrupt transformation. The previously sweet and agreeable child screams *No! Mine!* A sense of independence arrives and from then on, our beautiful but challenging world is seen from a selfish, personal perspective—what is good for *me,* what is dangerous to *me.*

"We are encouraged to grow up to be independent people—full of loving kindness—but in this independent human, there remains a subconscious uneasiness, an incompleteness, a feeling of not being *enough*—because we were not created to be alone."

Medina agreed, "The majority of our human history has functioned from this selfish thought process, with power struggles and acts of inhumanity as we fought over what should have been our Garden of Eden. This selfishness has caused a destructive impact on all forms of life on our planet, and even the Earth herself."

"It got worse in the 20th century," interjected Todd, "as man created more elaborate ways to take things for himself. Individual fear, greed and desire for power are the motivating forces behind wars and violence between countries, religions, and even down to personal relationships. The real root cause of these destructive tendencies comes from an individual feeling of separation and vulnerability, of being flawed and needing enhancement. Even in trying to be good, often the goal *really* is to be better than the next person!"

We were sitting around the long restaurant table still laden with empty coffee cups. I furtively leaned back behind Sonya and peaked at Mildred and her cronies. They were sitting silent. Mildred's eyes were wide and her mouth hanging slightly open, hanging on every word. The other two wore slight frowns of concentration as they took in the strange information and some perspectives that were completely new to them.

When we at the table compared beliefs, it became evident that all our religions acknowledged some version of the same collective mental illness—the illusion, the *delusion* is that each person is *alone* and not connected to God or to each other or to all of creation.

Sonya agreed and said "Hindus call it *'Maya,'* or the veil of delusion."

Todd's friend Takil—who turned out to be Buddhist—said "it is the world of suffering and misery, or *dukkha.*"

"The Kabbalah states that the knowledge of our connection to God was hidden in our subconscious at birth," added Rachael.

I thought a minute and said, "When Jesus spoke his first words to start his ministry, he said, in Mathew 4:17, *'Repent! For the kingdom of God is at hand!'* The word repent here, was a mistranslation. I have heard that the word Jesus used was *metanoya* and that has the same root as metamorphosis. Jesus was urging us to change like the caterpillar who has served his time on the ground, looking at life with near-sighted vision—to transfigure into the butterfly which can float up to see the whole inclusive picture."

I continued, "Jesus came to teach us to embody the Christ consciousness—to be 'born again' into the full awareness of the Oneness of all creation—to realize our unbreakable connection to God and to each other."

From what we were learning, it appeared this misconception—this false belief that we could be separate from God and each other—is addressed in numerous religious cultures. Many teachers had come to show us the way out, like Gautama (Buddha), Moses, Jesus and Mohammad. They all taught the same Truth.

"So, our teachers came to *save* us," concluded Todd, "To get us to look at the world differently, to wake up!" Everyone acknowledged that these teachers were not well received and when they were gone, their disciples and followers sometimes misinterpreted and narrowed the message until the religions became divisive entities, the exact opposite of the teachers' intent.

And yet, we agreed that in spite of the human mishandling, the *Truth* still shines through. We looked at each other and saw the shared similarities of *Spirit.* We saw dear people of sustaining faiths following their individual paths which seemed to be in pursuit of the same goal; **to remember Source—or God—and thereby remember the universal Oneness of all Creation, the Oneness of which we are ALL a part.**

I had watched Mildred throughout the talks to see how she was reacting to the discussions. She had a slightly confused look on her face at times, and a flash of anger would come and go, but she listened intently. When we spoke of the selfish attitudes of man, she nodded her head in agreement. When Jesus was mentioned she relaxed a little. When everyone disbanded I was relieved that nothing had "riled her up" and glad that she got to learn about the other religions in a non-confrontational setting.

Coca Leaf Tea

After the bus brought us back to the hotel, we packed for an international departure to Mexico in the morning. I had bought a little box of coca leaf tea for a dollar, from an eight year old girl, to show the people back home. Jack heard about it and came knocking on our door.

"Get rid of that coca leaf tea!" he exclaimed without even saying hello. *"Just get rid of it!"* Hands on hips, barely inside our door, he

stared me down. "We're going through customs in the morning so dump it! Okay?"

He remained standing in the door, unwilling to enter. Slowly he calmed down, switched gears and then asked, "Has your group had any more spiritual discussions like earlier today?"

"Yes, I guess we do a bunch of it," I admitted, while still feeling chastised.

"Is it alright if I join you sometime?" he asked.

"Of course you're welcome. We'll let you know, but we never know when they're going to occur." I agreed, although my bruised ego wanted to say, *"No! You tyrant!"*

He turned to Sonya. "I have a question to ask you."

Sonya responded, "Yes?"

He hesitated a little, "I didn't feel comfortable breaking into your discussions but I wanted to know…. Well, all this 'Oneness' talk you do is unsettling to me. Does that mean that after we 'get it'—that Oneness consciousness—and then someday die, that we will then melt into the ocean of God like drops of water and we disappear? The thing that is *us* just goes away—just adds its special part to the whole and is gone forever? That's not something I like to think about."

"My belief, after my out of body experience," replied Sonya, "is that we are then in unison with all of life. But we don't disappear into non-existence, completely absorbed into one consciousness. Each of us will remain in a state of self-perception, individuality for all eternity. And, as we reach higher awareness, each of us will be graced with the perception and understanding that we *complete* the Oneness, God."

Jack's face revealed a look of relief and happiness. As he turned to leave, he focused on me and his parting words were, "Dump the tea!" Satisfied, he left.

When he had gone, I finished packing and, out of spite, I considered hiding it, the innocent little box of tea, which looked like bay leaves. But finally, I threw it in the trash.

Later, was I ever *glad!*

Next morning at the airport, after the police thoroughly searched through all the luggage, they lined everyone up on the runway and two German Shepherd dogs spent ten minutes sniffing each of us thoroughly. Whew!

Buddhism

The flurry of customs behind us, our plane lifted off for Mexico and we settled in for a long flight. Medina pointed out that she didn't know much about Buddhism and asked Todd and Takil to give us a mini-class on the subject. We all couldn't stop comparing religions. Sonya reminded me to go get Jack, which I did.

"Well," began Takil, "Buddhism started as an extension of Hinduism—a *reform* initially, like Christianity to Judaism. But like them, it became a separate new religion eventually.

"We are Tibetan Buddhists, and as you know, each denomination gives a different slant to the picture. For us, even though life is dukkha—painful, dislocated, 'out of joint'—personal experience is the best teacher.

"The reason for this is that we humans have a consuming desire for *personal* fulfillment that overruns our lives. If we can embrace the whole picture, and notice that we are not alone in this craziness, we can be released and stop the pain."

"The same old selfish outlook, isn't it? So how do you go about curing that?" asked Rachael.

"We practice the fifty-nine mind training slogans called 'Lojong'. Their message states that we can use *everything* we encounter, pleasant or painful, to awaken genuine loving-kindness, compassion and a sense of belonging to the *Whole*. These teachings contain a very supportive meditation practice called *Tonglen*—taking in breath and sending it out."

I exclaimed, "I've used that practice for a long time—ever since I first discovered it in the book *Always Maintain a Joyful Mind!* It was written by a woman, Pema Chödrön, a Buddhist monk."

Medina asked, "Give us an example."

Looking at Todd and Takil, to see if they wanted to do it, I saw they were curious about my experience, so I explained.

"When someone I love is in a lot of pain, like after losing a spouse, I try to breathe into my heart all their suffering, anguish and grief, hold it there, and then breathe out love and compassion to them. I used it on myself when I lost my husband Ron. It helped. And, I've used it to try to 'heal the world,' by sucking in with my breath all the discord and strife, down into my heart, and then blowing out only peace and love. During the process, it seems that *my* heart is opened and softened as well. I receive what I give."

"It seems counterintuitive," Takil added, "To willingly bring *inside* ourselves the suffering, and then to let this experience break our heart open to its true nature of vastness, boundlessness. The hardness of suffering can dissolve into us, and then... the miracle! With our next exhale from this space of loving kindness, we can send out merciful peace."

Rachael interjected, "I've read that the heart has an electro-magnetic field that is sixty times more powerful than the brain's field. Scientists have recorded changes in other people's brain waves just by being *near* someone who is practicing heart compassion. It sounds like the heart has a mind of its own."

"Yes, yes! That's it!" exclaimed Takil. "Buddhism asks that you not try to run away from whatever pain is hurting you, physical or mental. Get closer to it, make friends with it. Make friends with whatever you perceive as *bad* in you or in others, and be generous with what is *good* or what you cherish. The goal is an awakened heart, one we already *have,* but couldn't recognize before."

Since the discussion seemed to be over, Jack got up to return to his seat and thanked us for including him. As he passed, I saw a bemused expression as his eyes searched my face.

CHRISTIANITY *"God's spirit is said to move over the waters as the will of artists moves over the material to be shaped by their art."*

Thomas Aquinas

17 Mexico

We found Villahermosa, Mexico, a thriving city of modern hotels and shops with lively, body-moving music pouring out of the doors. Open-air restaurants exhibited long slender fish impaled by cooking skewers, tantalizingly roasting right on the street to entice the passers-by. Street corner carts held slices of fresh coconut meat or mango to be sprinkled with chili powder. The Mexican joy of life, expressed as music, art and riotous color, overwhelmed our senses.

Upon entering the hotel, Jack introduced us to Miguel, our distinguished Mexican guide, who would give an expert introduction to Mexico and the Mayan people. Miguel proved to be much more than a guide as he had been a professor at the university for many years. His spiritual studies led him to leave steady employment and begin a life of sharing with visitors his passion for the Mayan history and their spirituality.

Everyone soon noticed that Miguel had a *presence* about him, a refusal to get stressed or rushed or upset in any way. He seemed very wise and exuded a great love of people. A young apprentice named José assisted him on our excursions.

The museum Parque-Museo La Venta was the first stop on our adventures the next morning. Relics were exhibited of the Olmec civilization that existed *before* the Maya. One very stunning artifact was a giant, round Olmec head about five feet tall. It had a broad nose, wide nostrils, and was made of dense brownish-black basalt.

Unexpectedly, Miguel had a strange request. We were each to place our hands on the head, one person at a time, and share any impressions or images that came to us. Reluctantly, after others had seemingly interesting experiences, I sidled up to it and mentally strained to "get something".

With some embarrassment, I shared my vision. "Well... all I saw were monkeys." Everyone laughed until Miguel took us over to several five foot long, thin, rounded stones that were lined up in a row. The Olmec worshiped *monkeys*, and those stone "bars" held them in their cages. My jaw dropped...

Next, we were to be the first "foreigners" allowed to experience and participate in a sacred Mayan ritual at a special waterfall. Jack forewarned the troupe that we would get very wet during the experience, and participation in this ritual was optional. He counseled the silver-haired ladies and anyone else who declined, to just watch from the bank of the stream.

The rest of us—having prepared ourselves with swim suits under outer clothing—each peeled down, and waded in one at a time. Medina and Sonya were more modest, so they had worn inexpensive clothing, to exchange for dry clothes later. Each person sat *on top* of a bubbling spring in the shallow pool facing the waterfall and held a wooden fish up to the falls.

Todd went before me and I thought I saw him wrestling to keep a straight face. When it was my turn I sat, trying to be respectful and grateful for the privilege of being allowed to experience this private, well-guarded ritual. I stifled a giggle when I realized that a "spring enema" might be quite possible! To make matters worse, the assistant, Jose, bent close to each person sitting on the spring and reverently blew into a conch shell. To my dismay, the sound that came out was sort of like a weak duck being molested. Managing to scramble up and stumble to the side, I then looked over at Todd and we were gone! Out of control with suppressed laughter—we both nearly split a gut, trying to be quiet.

Well, I soon paid penance for such sacrilegious thoughts because the next part of the ceremony was to walk barefoot through painful rocks to the falls and to lean both hands on the rock wall and hold my head and shoulders under the waterfall for a respectable time!

I couldn't walk to the falls, as my feet are horribly tender. But I crawled and stumbled to them anyway—there seemed no option, no mercy, for a sacrilegious soul—as Miguel just stood silently and then said, "Do it." It took me three tries until I held my head and shoulders under the excruciating ice water long enough—until I did it right.

Old soul, my patootie! Miguel is a sadist, and paying me back for my disrespect, I thought. Of course, everyone else did it perfectly, including Sonya. I regretted my attitude a thousand times, but… the devil made me do it. Surely the Mayan spirits must have giggled too, as they observed me making a spectacle of myself.

When we finished and got back on the bus, I heard Takil quietly trying to convince Todd to take these spiritual experiences more seriously. He bent close to talk privately to him. Mildred, in the seat across the aisle, leaned over (almost tipping into the floor), trying to hear what they were saying. She was continuing to act like a bird dog on point, searching for sin—the "sin" of homosexuality.

While driving the country roads, we saw cacao (chocolate) beans being dried in the sun. Chocolate comes from the fruit of a tree and the people place the beans in the sun to dry. We got to taste the fruit that looked like a small melon, but we were cautioned "Don't bite the bean."

Of course, I had to try. The bitter shock reminded me of tasting straight cocoa powder as a kid. But the *final* product, Mexican chocolate, is a rougher version than we were used to at home. Less filler (wax), less sugar, less fat, and less grinding yields a slightly sweet, more fibrous product—but so good.

We bought papayas and coconuts and sampled the coconut milk. The vendors were delightful and very proud of their produce. They had seemed to really enjoy my face as I bit into the chocolate bean.

At the end of the day we were given two options for the evening. Miguel offered a home-cooked meal at the abode of his friends or the exciting night life of Villahermosa. Our little band chose to stay with Miguel for an authentic Mexican supper. The rest of the group crowded around Jack, excited to go back to town. He was grinning and enjoying his troupe.

I watched him and realized that if he appreciated one or two of the women more than others that night *it wouldn't diminish my worth, my value, in his eyes or in my own.*

Even though selfishly, I still wanted Jack to pursue me, to prefer me, I looked at that rascal and loved him just as he was, lavishing the experience of the female like a dog relishes a good roll in fragrant spring grass (or even the odorous droppings *in* the grass). He would "bring the story home" with him. The dog would smell of his choices and Jack would add that night and its experiences to the persona of Jack.

Insights I had gained on this trip were helping me to make peace with my own wanderings through the male mystique (and population) and I was now able to gain a new perspective on that history. Just as I thought lovingly of Jack, I now was beginning to love and look fondly at *myself—even* the parts I had judged—*especially the parts I had judged.*

Jack and I had histories and experiences that made us fuller, wiser, and more compassionate with others—made us better equipped to understand and love the lusty, wayward souls we encountered in life. And that was where I always said I was headed—*to embody God's unconditional lovingness.*

When we approached the home where we were to have dinner, the husband and oldest son were working with two beautiful horses. We paused in the yard and watched with admiration as they put the horses through their paces. There's a rich culture of horsemanship in Mexico and it spawns some marvelous cowboys.

The wife joined us and stood with her husband. Our hosts, a young couple, were so proud of their new house. It was made of concrete blocks with a metal roof and had two rooms, one larger space to make the living and kitchen area, and a bedroom. The "inside" bathroom that they happily offered had a toilet with no seat. Common in Mexico, the bathroom tissue was to go in the trash can, *not* down the toilet.

I thought of how perspectives here could be so different from back home. These people felt so lucky, so grateful and proud to have an *inside* bathroom with running water in the house, and *one* bedroom for the couple and three children!

When we arrived, the wife had been patiently frying her homemade tortillas. We were captivated by the strange pungent aroma full of unknown herbs and spices that was coming from a big pot of what we assumed had chicken in it—due to the feathers we had encountered out in the yard.

Just as we were getting comfortable on a large over-stuffed red velvet couch and chairs, the electricity went off. Dusk had fallen outside and our room went pitch black. Calmly, the woman got a flashlight and went right on frying the tortillias. Her stove was a propane burner. Opening the back door and shining some car lights inside, allowed us to find the food. Interestingly, the family remained calm—no one was stressed. Apparently, power outages were a common occurrence here. If it had been *my* party, I would have been freaking out. I was impressed.

When the meal was ready, the children of the family came in from the bedroom to eat with us. They were full of happy energy but were quiet and well behaved. I sensed that the parents were very glad for the money we had supplied for the meal.

Rachael

After we said our grateful "good-byes" to our host family, we climbed back up on the bus. Rachael sank into the bus seat beside me. We were thankful to be going back to the hotel. She sighed deeply and said, "I have enjoyed every experience of this tour, but my age is slowing me down. I'm sooo tired!"

I agreed. "Me too. That bed is calling."

She turned slightly in the seat so she could face me and settled back in the flickering lights of oncoming cars. "It's hard to go without eating meat on this trip, but I have to, because none of it is kosher. I'm starving!" She had only eaten a few vegetables and the tortillas.

"Rachael, I am curious about you," I said. "From all you have told me, your spiritual concepts are very open, progressive and deeply mystical. We are drawn to you because of your inclusive, loving nature, but you also embrace a strict Hasidic sect of Judaism with its carefully observed laws. I don't understand. Talk to me!"

She nodded acknowledgement of her unusual faith. She smiled and admitted, "We actually have 613 sacred laws to follow. The root meaning of the word 'religion' is 'to tie back or bind'. Did you know that?"

"No, I didn't."

She went on, "In practice, religion can do just that—it can restrict us, bind us. Many a war has been launched over opposing points of religious doctrine. Just as devastating are the broken family relationships caused by harsh religious laws and judgments. Family members can be banned from the clan over a lapse of observance.

"Religion can bind us… or it can launch us to the Divine. Happily, my Judaism does both."

"What? I don't understand." I tried to see her face in the flickering lights.

"It's hard to explain my identity as a Jew although it's probably the largest part of me. Unlike some others of my faith, I embrace the idea of reincarnation. I believe I was a Jew in all my past lives and will be in the next ones. So I feel I have *lived* our painful history; on some level I remember it. This history is my unique gift to creation. So to live it well, to observe the laws that *you* see as restricting and confining, is binding but natural for me. I just *have* to do it to be authentic—to be who I am.

"The Hasidic portion of Judaism is known for deep study of its sacred writings—the Torah, the Talmud, the collection of Midrash and Kabbalah… I went from one orthodox community to another to study under a Hasidic Rabbi because he was dedicated to searching out any wisdom of God that he could find, examining every word or story, foraging through all the accumulated knowledge of the past, and even filtering through ongoing discourses between Jews today. We're *searching*. We're searching for God and trying to find the meaning in life.

"You may not believe it, but I have studied your 'Course in Miracles' for many years and we even meet in a Christian church.

You must be aware of the book, 'A Return to Love', by Marianne Williamson?"

"Yes. The book introduced me to the thought process of the 'Course' and caused me to go on to really study it."

She said, "Did you know Marianne Williamson had two great-grandfathers that were Rabbis? The 'Course' is inspired by Jesus, and Jesus was a Jewish prophet. It's the same Truth. I find no conflict.

"I believe that Jesus was the great exception to our human dilemma—the belief in separation. He demonstrated the Christ Consciousness with his life…and death… and that it is an attainable human condition. Jesus was aware that He and the Father were One and that <u>we also are joined in that Oneness</u>."

I sat back to take this all in. *This profoundly Jewish woman has a reverence for Jesus that is deeper than I had recognized.*

Rachael gestured toward the seat behind us where Medina was sitting (and likely eavesdropping on our conversation). "Medina *also* honors Jesus and his teachings and searches for God, but her goal as a Sufi is to *experience* God. She studies under her Sheikh, her spiritual guide, with that focus and it is so beautiful! Her practice of eating only kosher meat is difficult, too. She is very hungry tonight, just like me. I understand her and admire her path."

A small voice came from behind, "I *am* hungry."

Rachael continued, "Each of us is beautifully unique, one of a kind, like snowflakes—a perfect creation of spirit and nature.

The revered Hasidic Rabbi, Rebbe Mendel Schneerson, greeted thousands of people in one day—endless lines of souls seeking to meet him. Someone asked how he could hold up through all that. He said, 'How can I get tired of looking at *diamonds?* I think he saw individual precious jewels—diamond souls."

I looked at Rachael, a gentle, highly intelligent, and sometimes assertive soul, sitting next to me. I loved her! Every nook and cranny of her personality. Leaning over to pull her closer to my seat, I tucked her arm under mine and squeezed her hand. I thought, "*This is one of the joys of life, to recognize and appreciate a unique expression of the One—one expression in a million.*"

A "knowing" dawned on me as we bumped along the road in our bus. We are more than children of God. We are the very experience that Source is having of Itself, through us. Our lives are about the finding of God, the moving into the consciousness of God and then the spreading of that Divine Loving Energy.

Now, if I could just hold that thought for at least ten minutes, it would be a miracle.

CHRISTIANITY

"All praise be yours, my Lord, through all that you have made,
And first my Lord Brother Sun,
Who brings the day; and light you give to us through him.
How beautiful he is, how radiant in all his splendor!
Of you, Most High, he bears the likeness.

All praise be yours, my Lord, through Sister Moon and Stars;
In the heavens you have made them bright
And precious and fair...

All praise be yours, my Lord, through Sister Earth, our mother,
Who feeds us in her sovereignty and produces
Various fruits and colored flowers and herbs...

All praise be yours, my Lord, through Sister Death,
From whose embrace no mortal can escape."

Saint Francis of Assisi

---

18 Native American Spirituality

The next morning at breakfast, we were in for a special treat. Miguel introduced us to his good friend John, a member of the Oglala Sioux American Indians like the famous medicine man and spiritual leader Black Elk. John was a tall, broad man who surveyed the group with a wide, stoic face under long brown hair worn to his shoulders.

Choosing his words slowly and carefully, he leaned back in his chair at the table and told us about his Native Americans and their spiritual beliefs.

"Many may assume that the Red Man has no God because we don't give It a name. That is because *It's the unknowable power that is inside all of creation.* We believe the Holy, the Sacred, the *Wakan* doesn't need to be attached to a distinguishable supreme being. We *trust* in a sustaining order in all creation that we respect, protect and work alongside of. We believe that as humans we only own two things. While we live, we own our name and we own our power to choose. We can choose to love, to hate, to give pain or take pain away. There is no sense of the biblical concept of man's dominion over the earth and its creatures. We consider all things of creation to be our relatives—like Mother Earth, Sister Moon, Brother Sun and Brother Elk.

"It's often difficult for those who look on the tradition of the Native Americans from the outside, or through the 'educated' mind, to understand that no object is what it appears to be, but is simply the pale shadow of Reality. It is for this reason that every created object is Wakan, Holy."

Hearing his gracious wisdom, brought up a conflict of emotions. His belief, the Red Man's concept of the *All,* was my own! To honor nature and creation as sacred was second nature to me—to look for the Spirit within. In the past, I'd had no exposure to this beautiful Native American spirituality. In fact, I flushed with embarrassment at the thought of my inherited prejudice, the stereotype I grew up with of the primitive, ignorant, drunken Red Man.

My father worked for the Red Cross, after he retired from the Fire Department, and helped at the Native American Pow-Wows—their gatherings. There, he often encountered lice-infested children and horrible poverty. In his frustration, of not being able to make a difference, he judged them harshly and brought the concept home.

My thoughts returned to the room when Takil raised his hand to speak, "Please forgive me for the interruption, but I am amazed at your words! What you just said sounds like it came from the *Tao.* They seem to be identical. The Tao is the way of ultimate reality, and cannot be perceived or even clearly conceived of, because it's too vast for human rationality to understand. Above all, behind all, beneath all is the Womb from which all life springs and to which it returns. But, we see it as the 'way of the universe', the rhythm and driving power in all nature, the ordering principle behind all life. It assumes flesh and informs all things."

Common among Native Americans is a cultural tradition that no one interrupts the person speaking. That is considered impolite. John was silent for a bit, quietly absorbing what Takil told him, instead of being bothered by the interruption of his talk. "Your Tao is a very ancient religion too, correct?"

"Yes, very!" answered Takil.

John nodded and smiled in acknowledgement of the understanding they shared. Then he continued his talk. "I think that you will find common grounds between all the ways of worshiping the Wakan, the Holy. Our famous Native American spiritual leader and medicine man, Black Elk, also joined the Catholic Church. He found no reason that his spirituality and the Catholic Church were incompatible!

"Now I will tell you more that you probably didn't know. The way the Red Man lives is a very old, old way. Long ago a spiritual 'messenger' brought us a way of peace and a democratic process of government.

"There are no elections. Women choose the leaders, but consensus of the tribe must follow. We consider the Earth itself as female because without the female there is no life. Fundamentally, women carry the long view of life. Men seem to be more focused on the here and now. We learned a long time ago that men and women must work in full partnership because that is what it takes.

"You may think our religion is male dominated, because of our tradition of having male chiefs, but the women are the real 'power behind the throne'. The clan mother chooses a chief, a sub-chief, and two faith-keepers, male and female. The clan mother even has the 'power of recall' if the chief isn't doing his job correctly. She has a great deal of responsibility.

"Perhaps the most important characteristic of the Red Man is that sense of *mutual relatedness* which leads to the community-strengthening practices of 'mutual responsibility.' That concept is sorely lacking in Western culture. Did you know that the United States uses a hugely disproportionate share of the world's natural resources? "

John quoted an old Indian proverb:

"Treat the earth well: *It was not given to you by your parents, it was loaned to you by your children!* We do not inherit the earth from our ancestors, we borrow it from our children."

"For the Oglala Sioux to be the people we are meant to be, we are told to be thankful and to enjoy life. We are told to go to our sacred Black Hills and pray, through certain ceremonies, not just for ourselves but for the whole world. When we perform our ceremonies, it allows all creation to walk the soft Earth in a dancing manner together, and I think that is the responsibility we have. To simply sit and pray, without doing all those things that God tells you to do, is not to pray at all. It is what we call *howling in the wind.* When you honor the responsibilities that come with prayer, then you can bring out the song of the universe. That is a responsibility we all share.

"I am a Sun Dancer. Both women and men can dance. When we move to the music, we are seeking to take the pain out of the universe and to make the universe complete again."

Rachael recognized that John's people felt a significant weight of responsibility to perform their ceremonies—to positively affect the world. It was similar to her Jewish practice to celebrate the Holy days and rituals, observe their laws, and to pray frequently for the good of all. Interestingly, both cultures had experienced a "holocaust".

John continued, "The Lakota Sioux, in South Dakota, did not have to endure 'the trail of tears', that devastation forced upon the 'Five Civilized Tribes' of our American south. There, due to Andrew Jackson's Indian Removal act of 1830, most of the Native Americans were removed from the lands east of the Mississippi river—from Florida, North Carolina, Mississippi and Alabama. It was an ethnic cleansing that also included European Americans and African-American freedmen.

"The Native Americans had their children taken away to be 'saved' from their 'heathen' ways. Then they were forced to *walk* to reservations in what is now Oklahoma, and approximately one third died of disease, exposure and starvation along the way. The result was that twenty-five million acres of land was freed up for mainly white settlements.

"Many Lakota Sioux in South Dakota had our children taken away also, to be 'saved', forbidden to practice our rituals or even speak our language. Access to the Sacred Black Hills was forbidden, and today, we are required to get 'permits' to visit the land to have ceremonies. Of the 65 permits applied for, by varying organizations in a recent year, 62 were approved. We continue to be discriminated against, because only the three requests submitted by Native Americans were denied. Even a group of Hell's Angels got in. The age old prejudice is still in place. Until 1955 it was illegal for a Red Man to own land. You can read more about these things in Huston Smith's book, *A Seat at the Table.*"

John paused in sad reflection at this point, but then his face noticeably brightened. "Today, we Native Americans are often admired and our customs are copied by the 'new agers', especially after people read the book *Black Elk Speaks,* told by Black Elk himself. And yet, we can still be persecuted by the ignorant." John, now silent, looked us all over carefully as if to see where each of us fit in today's opinions of Native Americans.

There was an extended silence around the breakfast tables as each person appeared to think about his or her own ignorance of the Native American peoples. I was ashamed.

Finally summoning up some manners, we crowded around John to compliment his talk and knowledge of his Native American spirituality and culture, a culture that had instinctively balanced the male and female for centuries. We acknowledged that we just hadn't previously known the truth about the Red Man and were grateful to him for informing us. Not only had he just created some new Native American advocates, but he had shown us the common thread of Truth running through his spiritual beliefs and our own.

JUDAISM *"Have we not all one Father? Did not one God create us?"*

Tanakh Malachi 2:10

19 The Mayans

After the breakfast with John, we traveled to a little town that was having a religious holiday. Our tour group had been given special permission to come to the sacred event, but we were cautioned to be as inconspicuous as possible and not intrude too much on the festivities.

As we entered the lovely old cathedral, our senses were bathed with the aroma of burning incense and the hazy, streaming bands of light that fell from antique stained glass windows. The light fell on hundreds of long-stemmed flowers with the creamy blossoms filling the length of the stem. These flowers were scattered over the bare floor and the people of the village wandered along paths through the blossoms, to visit specific statues of saints placed along the walls. It seems that Catholicism and the native Mayan culture have blended into a very beautiful ceremonial religion.

Later that day, we were served a snack again, in a small home in town. While the husband stayed in the back, working with a horse and some goats, the mother and her oldest beautiful daughter proudly showed their hand-made textile art. The daughter knelt before a loom, placed on the dirt floor, and her shining dark hair fell across her face and back as she worked. She demonstrated how they inserted delightful patterns into the colorful lengths of hand-woven tablecloths and curtains and swatches to be hung on walls for decoration. All the while, the mother had a baby in her shawl on her back. The baby made no sounds, even when the mother made little tacos for us over a one-burner stove.

The humble home had two rooms, no inside bathroom, and the floors were dirt, and slanted downhill. I discreetly peeped behind a dividing blanket between bedroom and living space. Bunk beds around the walls accommodated four children and a double bed was there for the parents. Each person had a hook on the wall for their clothes. But somehow, the children were clean and neat and wonderfully friendly. Miguel whispered that the baby was older than it appeared and it had some sort of disability. Before saying our goodbyes, we bought some of the beautiful fabric art to show our appreciation for their hospitality.

The next day, after a two hour drive, we arrived at the Palenque National Park in Chiapas, Mexico. It was a lush, undulating land of steamy jungle and grassy hills. Butterflies, in a moving rainbow of colors, caught the sunlight. Joyously, they flitted through the giant elephant ears, palm trees and tall hardwood forests that were encased in mosses and creeper vines.

The day started with a ceremony. As we clustered around Miguel, he set out a blanket on which were placed sacred relics such as the 'melodious' conch shell. Spraying what smelled like rose water, he then honored the elements of earth, turning to face four different directions as he spoke:

> "Holy Earth
> Holy Water,
> Holy Air,
> Holy Fire,
> Holy Spirit."

Burning a bit of resin in a shell, he murmured prayers and blessings in the Mayan language. We didn't understand, but we thought it seemed to be honoring Creation and the All.

As we rose from the grass to begin our adventure, Miguel made it a point to get my attention. Silently he looked at me, his eyes burning with a purpose, a passion. I felt his great love of the rich heritage of this country and its people. He was laying it all out before us, and I saw how vulnerable his feelings could have been, especially as we passed the blue, undulating waterfalls that splashed through the park. He was giving me another chance. My previous sacrilegious attitude at the other waterfall seemed to be forgiven, and he once again was trying to show me his world.

We strolled through the park toward the ruins of the ancient majestic city. Then, Miguel stopped in a forested area and requested that we clear our minds and "hug a tree." I was impatient to see the ruins and had to consciously take a deep breath, to relax, and try to honor his purpose.

Hug a tree? Nothing's going to happen... Oh well, here goes... I looked around and chose a stately specimen and decided, after experimentation, that backing up to the tree was best and extended my arms around it behind me. I leaned back against the trunk, closed my eyes and rested my head against the rough bark. *Immediately, I was a tree!* I was aware of *roots* stretched deep into the soil and my *branches* reached up to the welcoming sky. My *leaves* were even caressed by the loving wind. The altered reality lasted for about 15 seconds and it was over. Nothing like that had ever happened before! Everyone else was still "hugging" and I was done.

Todd hurried up to me as we resumed the walk toward the ruins, "Jo, did you feel anything?"

"Yes!" I exclaimed. "It was wonderful." I couldn't, didn't *want* to describe my experience to him at that moment.

"Man! That was the coolest thing," he agreed. "I've always heard of 'tree huggers' and now I know why they hug." We shared our excitement and then joined the other folks to finally explore the various ruins scattered across the wide grassy hills. Eventually, our troupe arrived at the base of the most famous pyramid, the funerary Temple of Inscriptions.

Climbing lots and lots of steps was required to explore the pyramid. As I climbed higher and higher and watched my feet to ensure safe foot placement, I realized that the Mayans must have been very small people! The steps were extremely shallow, almost impossible to put a whole foot on. A bit later I discovered that *going down* was the trickiest of all. My descent had to be negotiated sideways and I imagined myself a bent-over crablike creature scuttling down the steep inclines.

Having just arrived at the bottom step, a scream behind me made me jump, and I turned to see Mildred *rolling* down the steps! Takil stopped her by grabbing her flailing legs—the parts of her body closest to him—and quickly pulled her skirt into a more lady-like position. Todd arrived, and reached out to cradle her head in his arms.

"Mildred, are you all right?" As she foggily stared up into the sky, he intently watched her and held her head steady while he explored her arms for injury, with his other hand. She had stopped rolling on one of the extra wide steps spaced evenly up the pyramid. "Mildred, you fell down the steps!"

"What?" She looked around as if trying to get her mind to grasp this astounding development. "I was just standing on that top…" She pointed one bleeding arm. "I guess I backed up too far."

Todd wouldn't let go of her head and, satisfied that she was flat on the landing, asked Takil to carefully move one leg and then the other to see if she flinched, could feel them, could wiggle her toes. Except for superficial scratches and bleeding, all seemed to be normal.

I waved frantically and called out to Miguel to get medical assistance and to notify Jack, who was on the other side of the pyramid.

Todd quietly said, "Mildred, your arms and legs seem fine, just scraped up, but I can't let go of your head because we need to keep it straight and still, till they check you out at the hospital." He bent close to her ear and his words and hands comforted her.

He stayed right with her after the stiff neck brace was in place and even climbed into the ambulance to accompany her to the hospital.

We waved goodbye. As the doors of the ambulance closed, Mildred was staring at his face with open gratitude and affection. I shook my head in amazement and murmured, "God works in mysterious ways to teach us about His love."

Heartened that Mildred would probably be all right after all, we returned our attention to the pyramid and prowled around in and out of the ruin, exclaiming at the beautiful stone carvings, the hieroglyphs that depicted the history of the Mayans and their ruler Pakal, who lived in the year 615 A.D. Miguel pointed out that the 'glyphs' were beautifully carved in a curling, rounded fashion, very unlike their Egyptian counterparts that were much more angular and straight edged.

Jack led us to some carvings that looked like men in space ships, wearing helmets with a breathing apparatus. We were amazed and thought the images supported the theories that the Mayans had extraterrestrial help. He worked his way through the group and was sure to point out the glyph that tracked the 5,125 year cycle of time that he would talk about later.

The best example of the beautifully carved hieroglyphs was found down inside the Temple, on the lid of the giant, stone sarcophagus of King Pakal. Jack said that when the tomb was opened in 1948, the ruler's skeleton was found to be wearing a jade mask. I finally understood why several vendors in the park were selling strange, curved, green stone masks. They were replicas of the original from the tomb.

As Miguel led the troupe down the steps toward the next ancient building, Jack lagged behind the rest. I stopped too, drawn to him. We were standing at the highest point, with the best view of the whole city.

The rest of the group turned a corner, disappeared, and we were left alone to survey the sprawling ancient Mayan city below, now bathed in a late afternoon rosy light. Standing together, as we had in Peru at the Temple of the Sun, this time, I felt him come up behind me and carefully place both of his hands at my waist. His warm fingers encircled my body gently, as if it were precious to him. Then he moved in closer until our bodies touched. His breath, near my ear, was ragged and heavy as he insistently squeezed my waist and pulled me closer. His head bent down and he nuzzled my neck.

My breathing increased, to match his. Any resolve to stay away from him melted away. I was his for the taking.

Then he left me... again.

The closing ceremony that afternoon was held behind the ruins as there were too many people still exploring the park, and we needed some privacy. Only about six of us chose to participate. Again, Miguel was loving and allowing, aware that his ceremonies would not be appreciated by everyone.

We sat around the little blanket and meditated. I 'saw' with closed eyes, many pairs of eyes looking back at me, of all shapes and sizes, some Asian, some round, some narrow-set—all kinds. They just looked back at me and I never did figure out what that was…

As we left the park, I caught up with Miguel. After briefly mentioning my extra-sensory experiences of that day, I asked him, "What were they, those unusual perceptions?"

"You felt a common phenomenon here around our ruins. There's an ancient, potent energy that seems to cut through the veil and give people experiences not available elsewhere."

He stretched out his arm and I felt his warm hand cradle my shoulder. Dark compassionate eyes focused on me with a palpable blessing of unconditional love. I had the feeling that his eyes could see right through me—could even see my raw longing for Jack. I felt completely transparent to him, but incredibly, only unconditional approval of *all* of me radiated from him. He offered congratulations for my being open enough to receive the messages that were given to me. He said, "I was just 'told' that Mother/Father God is well pleased with you, precious daughter."

I was humbled.

So many emotions rolled through me. That raw, sensual encounter of desire for Jack was still tingling in my body. And yet now, I was wrapped in the seemingly conflicted spiritual longing for an increased closeness and approval from God.

Did I have to choose one over the other? Were they opposites or part of the same thing? I believe that sexuality is a lovely God-given grace of life. So how could they be exclusive of each other?

In the next moment, my spirit leapt inside of me with the hope that I *was* good enough, that God *was* pleased with me—all of me. If Miguel could see me—my inner human sexual cravings and my sacrilegious attitude at his sacred Mayan waterfall—and still love me, how much more love was available from God, if I just opened my mind and heart to it?

The heat had been brutal at the ruins and Sonya and I sank into our cool beds for a rest before supper. My mind whirled around, becoming still at last with the belief that not only was I acceptable to God, but that I was more precious for all my idiosyncrasies and flaws that weren't even 'flaws' after all. The parts of me that I had hidden—had been ashamed of in the past— now seemed to be *valuable.* My soul now understood more deeply the pitfalls, triumphs and *value* of sexuality.

In that altered state I had another vision. Worthy, at last, I was ready to join closer to my Higher Self, my Holy Spirit. My new intention was to try to see all of life from that elevated perspective. A long stairway appeared before me, looking very much like the steep, Mayan pyramid steps we had just climbed.

I decided to climb ten steps up. *That* would give me a better perspective on life. So I did, but when I glanced down at life, the longing came to be much closer to my Higher Self, to my wise Spirit. So I turned and *ran* up those steep steps, impatient to get to the top.

The next image I saw was bizarre! It seems that whoever speaks to me still has a great sense of humor. I looked at myself and I had become a *candy bar*—a juicy, sweet, succulent candy bar! And those facets of me that I had just learned to love *were the best goody parts of the whole bar!*

So, there I was at the top of the steps, laid out like a fruity, nutty, caramel-centered candy bar, ready for my Higher Self. But, instead of a wise soul in white robes, I saw *chocolate... Chocolate!* —warm, yummy, melty chocolate that poured out over me. It slowly ran all down my sides and encircled and hugged me with sweetness and Unconditional Love.

And we were, at last, One.

That night at supper, as Jack got up to speak, he said, "We're so glad that Mildred was cleared at the hospital and has rejoined us."

She stood up, and as she patted her ample torso said, "The doctor told me that this extra padding I carry probably saved me from a broken hip."

With chuckles all around, everyone applauded her safe return.

Jack's Mayan Investigations

"You've probably heard a lot about the Mayan's world-changing prophesies written in 400 AD. The Mayan civilization reached its height in Mexico and Central America between 435 and 830 AD. These supposedly primitive people worked on seventeen *simultaneous* calendars, each recording a different aspect of reality. Their knowledge of mathematics and astronomy was so superior that our science is just now starting to catch up."

He bent down and retrieved a stack of pretty yellow paperback books and came around the tables to distribute them to us. Back at his podium he continued, "Astrology was also a science well developed by the Maya because of their knowledge and tracking of the planets of our universe. *They knew the planets had an effect on our personalities from birth and throughout our lives.* Your books are *The Mayan Calendar Birthday Book,* written by Mary Fran Koppa." He grinned, half joking about the subject we could tell he felt strongly about. "Have fun looking up your birthdays and reading about yourselves because the books contain information on what you hoped to accomplish in this life and what energies you were given to work with."

He looked out at us and, with a subtle squaring of shoulders, launched himself as if for battle, into his main topic. "I know this is going to be a stretch for you to believe, but according to Dr. José A. Arguelles in his 1987 book, '*The Mayan Factor: Path Beyond Technology*', our history has been shaped by an intelligently focused galactic synchronization beam, probably emitted from the Sun of Alcione, in the Constellation of the Pleiades.* He arrived at his conclusion by extensive scientific research which he supplemented with deep shamanic-like meditation. A huge transformation awaits us as we pass out of that beam!"

Twenty pairs of eyes were riveted on Jack. Exclamations and excitement passed through the crowd. Everyone looked at each other with questions and a lot of skepticism in their eyes.

Jack grinned and continued, "Yes, I know this is probably new to you folks, but Dr. Arguelles believes that the primary intention of the elaborate Mayan calendar system was not to measure *time* but to record the harmonic calibrations of this synchronization beam.

"We on Earth have been dealing with a carefully calibrated, intelligently focused, high frequency <u>time</u> <u>beam</u>.

"Each time period increased the capacity of our DNA and intelligence. Our minds have been in a slow but steady expansion and acceleration that is really a major upgrade in our evolution.

"But humanity has done this before!

"According to Dr Arguellas, we have just ended the *fifth* cycle of our Earth under the influence of this beam. Each cycle that measured the movement of our solar system through space, has been 5,125 years long. The fourth cycle included Atlantis, its rise and fall. Our fifth cycle started with the first dynasty of the Egyptians and ended with the year of the destruction of the twin towers in New York (2001).

"Each year of our cycle, the beam increased our ability to evolve from a primitive to a full-blown, technologically and globally communicating mass of humanity. On December 21, 2011 we began a major evolutionary upgrade in our planetary life process. We passed into our new 'super human' phase."

The room was silent as we wondered if he had gone too far, lost his credibility. He looked at our faces—the disbelief—and wasn't alarmed. It happened every time he introduced this theory.

Laughing, he agreed that we had a right to be skeptical, but continued, "This technological explosion of ours has happened *so rapidly* that the human consciousness hasn't been able to switch gears to the new reality—the concept of **one** humanity—not separated countries and cultures. Our spiritual evolution has not kept up with our advancements in technology.

"We're still caught up in the ancient survival tactics of competition and aggression. It has been *us* against them, *our* country against your country, *our* political party against your political party, *our* religion against your religion, and *our* race against your race! That thought process cannot continue, if we are to *survive* on our planet.

"A few years ago it looked as if we, too, might blow ourselves up like Atlantis." Jack looked out and saw a few puzzled faces among the other people who nodded in agreement. So he explained the most widely accepted theory of the destruction of Atlantis. "The common belief now, is that a few of the ruling, intellectual class of the advanced culture of Atlantis abused their power and knowledge of technology and accidentally blew up the continent with their experiments. So the remaining people of the world had to begin again, to climb up the ladder of a developing civilization once more.

"And we've done it. We have mastered the technology again and are at that same crossroads. Many believe there are enough of us who have changed our consciousness to compassion and love—a growing world culture that can manage to work together. We're almost to the tipping point of the *New Earth*. We just might make it this time!"

As I listened, I had grave doubts about how far the people of Earth have come. *Had a large enough portion of humanity reached the point of desiring peace?* A bizarre thought occurred to me. There was *one* thing that would bond together all cultures on Earth instantly, and probably stop the wars... We would become one Earthly humanity automatically if the UFOs and their aliens descended on us en mass—and scared the crap out of us! We would suddenly have another... "Other."

Extraterrestrial Assistance

Jack continued his talk. "Extensive research indicates that we've had lots of extraterrestrial help during our fifth cycle, the fifth attempt for humanity to evolve on this planet. '*They*' have been watching, nurturing and feeding us technology for thousands of years."

A generalized rustling of disbelief stirred throughout his audience. Most of them either denied the existence of aliens or believed the television and movie versions of fearful extraterrestrial invaders, bent on conquest and destruction.

Jack saw he had lost a good portion of his audience. There was a murmuring dissension within the group. I checked our little band and found that we were open and interested in his theories, but some of the others had shut down—unwilling to even contemplate the possibility that interactive aliens were here, now.

"OK, I see some of you are uncomfortable with this information. Of course it is your choice. Could you just hear me out and quietly look at the possibility—what *if* there is some truth to these theories?"

The conversations quieted down, and he saw that he could continue, "Many believe that the ideas, the bursts of knowledge that led to new technological advancements were given by something or someone beyond our Earth inhabitants. I am suggesting that extraterrestrials might have helped along the way. But you don't give a gun to a baby. We have to grow up and become *responsible* enough to earn the next level of technological information. The extraterrestrials can't do it *for* us. *We* have to stop competing and fighting and rise in our spiritual evolution to the concept of 'oneness' or we'll get off track too, and end up like Atlantis."

No one wanted to speak... Jack stood there in front of us, searching our faces, waiting for a reaction to his words.

Rachael broke the silence, "I can't get my mind around that galactic beam business very well, but I do like the idea that our violent history of atrocities was just a symptom of our human growing pains—errors—in evolving to a better humanity, a more peaceful world."

"The thought of extraterrestrial help is comforting," I said, "that we are being watched and assisted into the next phase of our existence. I already felt ET's were friendly. I've been reading some books by Dolores Cannon, who's an author and regressive hypnotherapist. For twenty-five years, she has been regressing people who claim they were abducted by aliens. She says in all that time, *no-one* who was deeply hypnotized, has said the aliens want to *hurt* Earth's inhabitants—to take over our world. They just want to help us. They even told one abductee that we hurt *ourselves* more than anything *they've* ever done.

"I think there are probably many expressions of Creation unknown to us—populations of intelligent beings that have been waiting and hoping we would eventually overcome our fearful, combative mentalities *and finally join them in the peaceful universe.*"

Todd took it a step further, "We may be called on to *carefully* get to know these new neighbors—to accept and integrate them into our reality instead of going into fear and trying to shoot them out of the sky. Trouble is, our movies and television have thrived on the manufactured fear stories, stories we have been fed for years and years. It will be hard to change our perspectives, to drop the fear."

Medina spoke up. "Jack, you've presented us with a tremendous amount of scientific information in a short time, and a lot of mind-bending theories. It'll take me a while to think about it all. But my mind gets stuck on a question. Where is God in all of this? Our idea of creation is expanding every day!"

While our minds were still filled with turmoil over his last information, Jack presented us with more.

Divine Integration with Humanity

"Dr. Amit Coswami, Professor Emeritus from the University of Oregon, a pioneer of the science of consciousness and an expert in quantum physics, says after a lifetime of scientific exploration, he has a new view of spirituality.

"His father was a guru in India and he, like Dr. Arguelles, combined science with years of deep meditation. He now says the Divine is integrated within us—not separated from us—integrated into our whole Earthly life. Dr. Coswami says, 'Separation of the sacred from the mundane is hurting our civilization. Any creative thought is Spirit mixing with life or matter.'"

John, our Native American friend, jumped up and strode to the front. "I'm glad you scientists are finally getting the idea! We Red Men have been saying the same thing for generations. *Everything* has the Wakan—the One who has no name—living in it. The spiritual dimension pervades every moment, every action. We are living in the Presence of the Creator. All time and all things are holy!"

Todd stood up and jauntily placed his hand on his hip. "John, you *know* that Takil told you our Tao shares the same viewpoint as your Native American one."

Takil chimed in, "Yes, you *know* that Brother John." The room responded with a swell of happy laughter.

Rachael, not to be outdone, strode to the front of the room and putting her arm around John's waist, because he was so tall, looked up into his face with an affectionate grin and said, "Oh no, Brother John. You don't have a monopoly on that concept. Mystical Judaism through the Kabbalah has taught for centuries that there's nothing in creation that *isn't God!*" From the back of the room the Jewish couple waved their arms and shouted, "Hear! Hear!" More laughter erupted around our tables.

Medina called out, "Allah says in the Koran that 'Not heaven or Earth can contain Me, but the heart of a believer can!' God is in the spiritual heart of the believer, right here, right now!"

The two Muslim couples exclaimed, "Listen, listen, Brother John!" They clapped their hands in agreement and one tapped her water glass as if ringing chimes. It caught on, and more glasses sang out their songs of joy.

I wanted to add my religion, so I stood at my table and said, "Our Christian Saint Francis saw *through* creation to the spirit within—to the relatedness of us all."

The two Christian couples and our lovely silver-haired ladies pounded their tables, causing the empty supper dishes to bounce and rattle, adding to the fray. "Yes, Yes! We've got it too."

Mildred, overcome with emotion, stood up and shouted, "The kingdom of God is at hand! *We are all made in the image and likeness of God!*" Then she realized what she had just said. She sat down—looked a little confused—and after a few moments a big smile lit her face.

The joyous bedlam died down slightly and one of the pretty young ladies of our group, the sexy Rita, stood up and said, "When I started on this tour I considered myself an agnostic. None of the organized religions made any sense to me." She glanced at her Christian parents out of the corner of her eye and nodded, "I'm sorry... but yes, agnostic. However, this new concept of God in *all of creation* is a 'no brainer'. I get it! I want to find God from that perspective and I think I can swallow it whole without getting something stuck in my throat."

More laughter, noise and excited conversations filled the room. Everyone was talking animatedly with each other.

Amid the bedlam that filled the room, I strained to look around at the faces of Rita's parents. I could see the glazed look in their eyes. They, and other orthodox group members of the different faiths, had been presented with too many challenges—challenges to their concept of God and all the talk of ET's only made them appear uneasy, scared. I expected they would retreat back into their individual faith systems, and I hoped they would. There was peace to be found for them there.

Jack, reading the energy in the room, decided he was done. He performed a mock bow and left the podium to come to sit between Sonya and me—to make a sweet comical drama of snuggling between us.

Even with the distraction of Jack, the hairs raised up on my arms as I 'saw' with a new transparency, the spirit gliding joyously or quietly through each personality, flickering at me.

I realized on a whole new level that all of us were very cleverly disguised souls. Souls come to Earth thinking we were alone—to figure out the puzzle and to make the astounding discovery for ourselves—*that our spirits were created in the image of God's perfection and are forever, infinitely connected!*

Miguel's Maya

Miguel, with a great big grin plastered all over his face, strode to the front to speak, "You people are already seeing the Truth I came up here to tell you. The Mayan people are the same in our beliefs." Then his smile shifted to a more serious expression. "Each of our religions has taught us the Way, but we sometimes forget it.

"Did you know that many, many of the ancient religions and cultures contain a flood story, a history of total destruction with only a few survivors to carry on and start over? Europe's Greeks, Romans, Celtic and Turkish cultures have a story. The Near East, with its Sumerian, Egyptian, Babylonian, Hebrew and Islam cultures tell the tale. Russians, Hindus, Tibetans and the Chinese of Asia have the flood myth in their past. Brother John might tell you that the

Ojibwa Tribe of North American tells of a former world destroyed by water, as do the Muisca people of South America."

He looked around the room and then spoke, "Now I will tell you our story... Who were the Maya? Where did they come from?

"Señor Zamna, the Father of All, was one of the most holy and wise priests from Atlantis. He was told to leave Atlantis with a few good and wise men and go to the new land to start again, because their former home would soon sink. He did as told, and they came to the land of Mayab, today Yucatan. The name 'Mayan' translates to the 'Chosen Ones'. There they built the beautiful temples for worship and the cities of Izamal, Chichen Itza and more.

"Senor Zamna taught the native people of the Yucatan about astronomy, mathematics, calendars, the recording of the stars in the sky, and how to work with the Earth and its elements—basically how to love and respect Nature and to work with all living beings.

"The prophecies of the Maya were written as a warning to us, *us*—here and now! *Somehow they knew, even back then, that in our times, Mother Earth would be threatened as a result of man's mental imbalance, irresponsibility and lack of harmony.* They knew Kaban— the being of the Earth—would start a process of auto-purification for the Earth to heal itself using 'natural disasters.'

"Mayan Masters knew that the Pleiades Constellation influences, in an important way, the physical, emotional, mental and spiritual behavior of humankind through energies on our Earth. Jack told us about that synchronization beam that changes and evolves us. It is a beam that is emitted from the Sun of Alcione, *in the Constellation of the Pleiades.*"

Now, again, there was a rustling within his audience. We were being asked to accept essentially the same concept that Jack had presented to us earlier. We could see that Jack's scientific mind and Miguel's spiritual mind were in agreement.

"In the last years, our Sun has generated intense solar rays, causing high levels of radiation and great agitation in many living beings. We have to adjust to this new energy and people are asking themselves, 'Who are we?' 'What is our purpose on Earth?'

"There is a way of 'being' that is harmless and yet immensely powerful. The Earth is changing, not as a punishment but as a great opportunity to rectify our conduct, to elevate our consciousness, and amplify our love and respect towards all living beings on our Earth.

"*Everything is Holy!*" The usually quiet Miguel nearly shouted. "Everything is provided by the great Creator of the universe, the Father/Mother God.

"Each of *your* religions has taught that all creation is related— Spirit/God in matter—but, so much of humanity has lost that understanding."

Transcendent God

Miguel continued, "When mankind's collective consciousness shifted from a matriarchal understanding of the world as a living, sacred being, the Divine became a transcendent God, living in heaven. Patriarchal consciousness excluded God from the natural world—a world whose darkness man then had to conquer. Man thought he had dominion over things of Earth—it was for his taking, plundering, and humanity chased after the joys of materialism.

"Of course, there were those in each religion that knew the truth, but their protests were not heard. Within the indigenous spiritualities, the feminine influence was still intact and they, like the Native Americans, never lost their reverence for nature.

"We must get back to the consciousness of relatedness—to remember that we are all part of a Whole—God, mankind and all of creation.

"You women have the feminine impulse to recognize and *feel* the distress of humanity and Mother Earth. You also know how to nurture and to *heal*. Join with your men to make *harmony, love* and *respect* a social and political force. You can impact religions, cultures, economies, governments and the world. Please... Do!

"Who are you? Who are we?" he asked. "We are creators able to think and create. That is God's legacy to us. We must turn our heart lights on, the light of God inside. We must pour loving positive energy out to all creation."

As we finished for the evening we saw the two perspectives of scientific Jack and mystical, spiritual Miguel and their knowledge blended flawlessly.

Jack had been so intelligent and so handsome up there. His presence beside me was an irresistible draw. When he made it plain he wanted me with him again, I happily agreed but said it had to be the next night because Sonya seemed to need me this evening.

Sonya

Earlier that day, Sonya had climbed all those pyramid steps with the youngest of us, but I could tell she had not totally recovered from our Ecuador stomach illness. She still had her beautiful spirit shining through but it was wilting a little around the edges.

We went to our room after supper, climbed into bed together, and talked about her husband. He had been her wonderful companion for many years and they had raised a daughter and son together.

Their main purpose had been accomplished—to build a spiritual community that recognized the divinity within each person, no matter what religion or lack of religion they held. There was an orphanage, a soup kitchen, and temporary rescue housing for families. It was still being managed by two of the orphans they'd raised.

Sonya said, "Now, I feel great satisfaction at having lived life to its fullest. We accomplished so much and, without him, I feel a little bit at loose ends. My life feels quite complete... but I'm still here... so I'll happily go with whatever comes next."

I snuggled up closer and reached out to stroke her soft brown hand. "Love pours out of you Sonya. It's just what I needed to pull me out of the emotional pit I was in. Do you have any idea how much I love you? I'm so grateful that we met." I forcefully shoved down the nagging ache she had caused by my exclusion from her book writing. It felt like I was still being punished, because she wouldn't work on it around me, or mention it at all. I told myself, *It doesn't matter!*

"Our friendship is divine order," Sonya said. *"All that should be, comes to us.* You and I will be lasting friends from now on—we were probably friends before this lifetime, don't you think?"

"Has to be. Our connection is too close. It has to be," I agreed.

We were facing the end of our tour, the "Trip of a Lifetime". I said, "With today's technology, we can 'Skype' each other no matter where we are. We *have* to stay close—we *will* stay connected."

That night I had a very disturbing dream, a nightmare in fact. I reluctantly told Miguel about it the next day at breakfast.

"In the dream, I was looking down into a body of water. There was a group of maybe six large white fish, more like little whales. One fish was swimming around and each of the others was taking bites of flesh from its back. But that fish just kept swimming around, frisky and happy, all stripped of a lot of its body."

Miguel said, "You have just experienced a 'white dream'. Dreams where you notice the 'whiteness' of something significant in the dream, are spiritual dreams. The fish in your dream were white. I believe the spiritual message was that the companions of that fish were stripping away old energy and attitudes that did not serve it any longer and it was better off for the help."

Finishing my breakfast, I pondered on his words and became aware that I was, indeed, shedding old illusions and the ignorance that I had held all my life of the beauty of other cultures. But there were also valuable additions, psychological and spiritual gifts—gifts given from several of the people on this tour, especially from my precious Sonya.

But then, that same precious Sonya, grabbed my arm and dragged me to our room to prepare for our next big adventure—the cave!

20   The Cave

The next day the hotel supplied little knapsacks of sandwiches, fruit and chips with bottled water for each tour member. A picnic was planned during the exploration of a famous cave full of stalactites and stalagmites. We were to picnic in the great Cathedral room underground and were strenuously cautioned to bring every crumb back out—no littering!

More ruins were scheduled for that afternoon. Miguel informed us that Mexico has more than 3000 Mayan sites that are still covered with dense jungle and yet to be explored because there just hasn't been funding for excavation.

Our group arrived at the park early and thus had the place to ourselves. Excited, we trekked up and down the hilly path swinging our knapsacks beside us. After about thirty minutes of 'trekking', Rachael asked the local guide, "How much further to the cave?"

"We're about half way there," he said.

She stared at him in disbelief. "I have a blister on my heel already. If I'd known how far it was, I would have asked for a golf cart—or even a donkey!"

I covered my mouth, but laughter exploded out anyway. The thought of buxom Rachael bouncing along on a donkey was too much.

Rachael turned to Jack, "You should have warned us!"

Jack flushed, caught in an oversight. "The people who recommended this cave never mentioned the long walk to the entrance. I've never come here before."

I gave Rachael my emergency Band-Aid and we decided to make the best of it. Sonya was grateful when I offered to carry her heavy knapsack.

The path wound deeper and deeper into a maze of several small mountains. Finally the cave mouth materialized and, as usual, Sonya was the first in line to go in. We were told by the guide that there were lights and directions prominently displayed in the cavern, so strolling at our own pace was encouraged.

As promised, the pretty lights led the way, even shining different colors on the formations of interest. We paused at the first stalagmite which was bathed in blue light.

Sonya exclaimed, "Listen! You can hear the drops of water coming out of the limestone ceiling. Look at this stalagmite. It was formed over eons of time—drop by drop—and it comes almost up to my waist." She put her finger out to catch a drop, to taste it, and raising her tiny shoulders, shivered in ecstasy. "Oh, it's so *pure*. It probably started out muddy surface water before a tortuous trip through these mountain rocks, to come out here, clear and *perfect*." Something about the mountain's purification of the water struck a chord in me. Often, it takes such a journey to make something clear.

We had only been in the cave a short time and not yet to the famous Cathedral Room, when the floor started undulating under our feet! A wave of nausea hit my stomach.

Confused, I reached out for the wall to steady myself and the lights went out... Then I heard what sounded like chunks of ceiling collapsing somewhere around me. Dust roiled up into my eyes and nostrils. I tried to reach forward to Sonya. Choking from the dust, I fell into a spasm of coughing. In desperation, I pulled the neck of my shirt up over my nose and mouth.

All right Jo, I coached myself, *Take great gulps of this filtered air and yell!*

"Sonya... **Sonya!**" I screamed in panic. My hands searched blindly in front of me for her. I found only a rough rock wall. Disoriented, I reached out to one side and then the other, to find only the walls of the hall we had been following. A spasm of coughing overtook me again, and then my fingers explored forward to find a rough rock blockade where the hall should have been. *Oh God, Sonya! I have your knapsack and you don't have any food or water!*

Involuntary whimpering escaped from my lips and almost obliterated some muffled coughs behind me. I yelled into the blackness, "I can't find Sonya!"

Rachael called back, "We're trapped! The exit was blocked."

My hands shook so hard—clumsy—as I tried to touch the rock in front of me. There seemed to be one giant rock with other small rocks around it. I dropped to the filthy floor and groveled back and forth, sightless, trying to find an opening through the impasse and continued to call out, "Sonya!"

That is when I found her hand—her little hand. Searching to see how far I could trace it back, the reality sunk in. *Sonya was trapped under that massive rock.* I frantically tried to find a pulse—none.

Collapsing, I just rolled over and vomited, with spasm after spasm of spontaneous heaving.

"Jo… *Jo!* Are you there?" called Medina.

I wanted to stay on that dirt floor forever. Reality was too painful. But, I reluctantly crawled over to lean against the wall and answered her, "I'm here…"

She blindly searched above my head with her hands, before she found me sitting on the floor. "Rachael is okay." Grasping my arm she succumbed to a fit of coughing and then asked, "Where is Sonya?"

"Gone…" I moaned. "The ceiling collapsed on her and I found her hand sticking out from under the biggest rock." Saying it out loud helped me to comprehend that she really was *dead.*

"Sonya! Oh No... No... not Sonya, no! Are you sure?" Medina cried out in pain and disbelief.

With calls back and forth, Rachael found us in the dust-filled blackness and we clung together, sobbing and coughing, overwhelmed with fright and grief. Her hands searched in the dark, taking stock, and she realized Sonya wasn't there. "Where is Sonya?" she demanded.

"She's dead, Rachael. Under the rocks in front of us!"

"No! That can't be! *Where.* How can you be so sure? Show me!"

Reluctantly I struggled up from the dirt floor and pulled her to the blockade.

"Bend down Rachael," I said. My hand circled her wrist and after I found Sonya's hand, I pushed Rachael to touch the motionless, cold proof.

A spasm traveled up Rachael's arm and she jerked away from me. A tortured moan wrenched from her, "no... no... Oh God! No! Why Sonya? Why?" The horror overwhelming her, she reflexively, abruptly, tried to run away from the proof and me, and blindly crashed into the far wall of the cave.

Frightened for her, I searched the dark to find the lump that was Rachael, collapsed and sobbing on the debris-covered floor. Medina silently moved to us, drawn by the sounds of grief. We huddled on the floor, devastated... touching and comforting and trying to comprehend the tragedy.

After a while the dust seemed to settle. We could taste the dirt in our mouths. In the total silence, Rachael seemed to draw herself together, and ever-practical, she remarked, "We have some food and water."

"And… I… I have… Sonya's knapsack," I sobbed.

"We barely got started exploring the cave," Medina said. "It'll be easier to get us out… I hope we didn't lose anyone else."

Our prison was forty feet of hall between rock blockades. On the other side of the immovable entrance rocks, we began to hear muffled voices.

Encouraged by the sounds, we started to scream for help and then waited for a response. The sounds we heard were too weak to understand.

"But, they are there! If we can hear them, they can hear us," Rachael said. "They'll go get help."

That thought gave us some hope and we took turns calling to the outside until our voices gave out. Then, it was time to sit back against the walls and try to adjust to our new reality. What a difference possibly thirty minutes had made in our lives.

After a long, lonely silence, Rachael said, "You know, she's probably watching us."

"Who?" Medina asked.

"Sonya," I answered. It gave a breath of comfort to think of her as she had been in her earlier near-death experience—*watching the drama below, feeling no pain, feeling FINE.* She could see us—was able to feel our anguished love for her.

Difficult in the dark cave to keep track of time, perhaps an entire night had passed. We couldn't know for sure, but the voices had stopped for a while. Irrationally, I felt abandoned.

Suddenly, the floor started to tremble! We grabbed each other in panic. *Oh no, not again!* Then it abruptly stopped.

"I think earthquakes have after-shocks and they're not usually as strong as the original quake," Medina said. Several minutes later, another round of trembling scared us once more.

Our voices blended in frantic, whispered prayers.

Afterward, all was quiet.

Finally, there was a tiny drilling sound.

"Yaaaaayy!" Cheering erupted from our throats. After what seemed to be hours and hours, a small 'bit' popped into the cave.

It retreated and a tiny pipe replaced it, down on the floor in the wall beside the fallen rocks. A voice called, "Are you in there?" It was Miguel.

"Yes, yes, we're here! Medina, Rachael and me, Jo. But Sonya is dead. She was crushed in the earthquake."

His voice trembled, "She's gone? Are you sure?" He sounded devastated. His voice became muffled when he turned from the pipe and it mixed with other voices relaying the news back down the passage to the outside. Apparently the others were safe.

Then he informed us of the rescue plans. The engineers said that a small round tunnel, just big enough to pull us out, would be drilled in the solid wall along the side of the fallen rocks. They wanted to leave the caved in rocks in place to continue to support the rest of the ceiling. It would take them maybe one or two days, they would pump fresh air in through the tiny pipe, and run a plastic line to fill our water bottles.

Thankfully, there were no more after-shocks and we began to adjust, to tolerate being in the cave. Hope built in our hearts that the ordeal would soon be over.

Shabbat

Our appetites started to return and the knapsacks became a source of interest, a challenge, as we tried to figure out what we had to eat. Rachael cautioned us to save some for later, so we portioned it up. She then asked if we would share Shabbat (Sabbath) meal with her, to honor and remember God.

Because the earthquake happened on Thursday, we agreed that it must be Friday. Sabbath begins at sundown on Friday, so we made a little circle in the dark and Rachael told us she would say the blessing for lighting the imaginary candles, one for each of us, and one for Sonya.

> *"Barukh atah*
> "Blessed are You, Lord, our God, King of the Universe
> Who has sanctified us with His commandments and
> commanded us to light the Shabbat candles."

Then, she asked us to drink our 'wine' using the water bottles, and said,

> "Blessed are You, Lord, our God, King of the universe,
> Who creates the fruit of the vine."

She continued prayers over the meager Shabbat meal.

> "On this day, let us keep for a while what must drift
> away.
> On this day, let us be free of the burdens that must
> return.
> Let us learn to pause, if only for this day.
> Let us find peace on this day.
> Let us enter into a quiet world this day.
> On this day, Shabbat, abide.

"Entrances to holiness are everywhere. The possibility of ascent is all the time, even at unlikely times and through unlikely places.
There is no place on earth without the *Presence.*

"My soul came to me pure, drawn from the reservoir of the Holy. All the time it remains within me, I am thankful for its thirst for compassion and justice.
Let my eyes behold the beauty of all creatures;
Let my hands know the privilege of righteous deeds.

"How do we know when night ends and the new day begins?
Perhaps the new day begins when we can recognize the face of our brother or sister."

Rachael paused and added,

"We offer thanks to You, Adonai, for saving us from death by the earthquake, and we offer thanks to You for the gift of Sonya's life with us."

Time seemed to pass so slowly and our spiritual discussions started up again, partly as an extension of the Sabbath meal prayers, and partly to keep our minds occupied and calm.

My Jewish Heritage

I picked up where we left off, "I read in the past of several spiritual beliefs that stressed the unimportance of this carnal, human life compared to the *real, spiritual* world occurring on the other side. My heart rebelled at discounting this beautiful gift of being human. There is a good reason—a great purpose—in my being here. *I'm sure of it!*"

Rachael responded warmly, "Your Jewish heritage spoke to your heart. Jesus was a Jew and knew that God created the world and it was *good!* We refuse to consider the physical aspects of existence to be defective or unimportant. Marriage and sex are good. Possessions are good. Being both human *and* Spirit is *good.* <u>There is Divine purpose here!</u>"

I smiled in the dark. "So that's what it was, my Jewish heritage! You know… I think Jesus *could* have been the *unifying* factor between our three faiths. All three religions recognized the greatness in Jesus—the personification of our spiritual connection with God and with each other.

"The Christian belief that we are children of God has demonstrated our relatedness to God for generations. But it appears we <u>all</u> really do act like human children in relation to God, fighting over the love of a parent, believing that there isn't enough for everyone."

Medina said, "We carry, within our spiritual hearts, a mirror that reflects the qualities of Allah. We've dirtied and dulled our mirrors with the emotions of hate, pride, selfishness and greed. It's time to clean them off, shine up our mirrors with love, compassion and generosity. I'd love to see us learn to **share** our precious Jerusalem with our brothers and sisters."

Rachael added, "The Kabbalah teaches that the ultimate purpose of this long search for 'enlightenment' isn't just for personal soul growth. It's to enable us, when we're called upon, to say the right word at the right moment. All this work we do, studying, living, and enduring 'lessons' is so that we can utter the correct sound, make the right gesture, take the right action at the perfect time. This delicate moment requires a lifetime of improvement and practice of self-mastery."

She snickered, "God would like us to *'get **on** with it.'* He expects a return on His investment!"

We each smiled in the dark.

Time dragged on.

"Christians have a favorite hymn, 'Amazing Grace,' that has always puzzled me because of the second verse," I said. "I've been thinking about this cave tragedy, and that verse."

> *"T'was grace **that taught my heart to fear,**
> T'was grace my fear relieved,
> How precious did that grace appear,
> The hour I first believed."*

"How can we see the grace of God, when it comes, more clearly than out of tortured eyes and hearts full of fear? We think fear tears us apart and grace heals us, but *fear* is an integral part of the loving process. It's grace, too."

Heart in Remembrance

The drilling continued, day and night. We were grateful, but the sound vibrated our brains and practically turned them to mush. That, and the never-ending cold and hunger, grated on our nerves.

In a rare period of silence Medina said, "Muslims are called to *remember* Allah many times a day, no matter what activities are happening. My Sufi meditation practice, Q*albi dhikr* means *heart in remembrance.*

'I get quiet in meditation and listen to my heartbeat. It sounds like 'lub *dub* lub *dub*.' Then I start to say in my mind or out loud, 'Al *lah*, Al *lah*,' in time with my heartbeat. In the Koran, Allah says 'When you do my *dhikr,* I am remembering *you.*'"

Attracted to her practice, I asked, "Why don't we try it with you, Medina?"

She agreed to lead and we began. Initially, it was tricky as I couldn't hear my heartbeat and had to feel my pulse. Plus, our hearts were beating at different speeds. But we noticed our hearts slowly synchronized with each other and we gradually moved into a steady rhythm of "Al *lah,* Al *lah,* Al *lah.*" It was an emotional experience and brought a peaceful feeling inside… an assurance.

Later I said, "The longing for God is so powerful in humans. I think that the 'remembering' of the God we knew before birth is a key to life here on earth. To find our way back can be difficult, but I believe we're given clues. I think that whatever spiritual path individuals see before them was placed there to start that remembering. If the path nurtures that reconnection with God, if the small voice inside senses the authenticity of the way and there is a lifting of spirit and a yearning to know more, and if it engenders peace, not aggression, and doesn't condemn other paths or spiritualities as wrong, it could be the true path for that person. The heart will know."

We had finally tuned out the drilling sound. It had become comforting 'white noise', a symbol of our imminent rescue. Having been lulled into complacency, we were startled when the cave began to shudder and move. It was slightly nauseating. Debris and dust enveloped us once more and we panicked and whimpered, "Not again!" I broke out in a cold sweat, shaking like the ground beneath my feet.

My mind whirled. *Maybe the vibration of the constant drilling was making it more dangerous. Being so close to rescue, only to be crushed to death anyway, was just not fair!*

We felt so incredibly *vulnerable*—gradually wearing down in our resistance to panic—very close to completely losing it.

Medina shouted to get our attention, "Please do my heart *Dhiker* with me again. Let's remember God—experience Him!"

"My heart is *fibrillating . . .* but I'll try to do your Dhikr." I shouted back. Then I convulsed in a spasm of coughing from the boiling dust.

No rocks fell on us.

It was so hard to concentrate—to fight down the panic—but we kept trying. Shirts pulled up over our noses and mouths to combat the polluted air, we huddled together and started the chants.

Al *lah*, Al *lah* Al *lah*, we breathed in beat with our hearts.

Another rumbling caused the volume to increase from our throats.

"Al lah, Al lah, Al lah....! AL LAH, AL LAH, AL LAH!" We practically screamed the words to God... and it helped. Gradually, the panic that paralyzed our minds was diluted, subdued, by an unexpected power that came from the heart. Against all mental reasoning, we were comforted.

Silence enveloped us again and I noticed the drilling had stopped. The rescuers must have been aware of our danger.

After an extended period of silence, Medina whispered, "My precious friends, when we joined our voices and cried out to Allah

together, it broke down all my barriers to the Beloved. I surrendered everything, my hopes, my dreams, and the future with my family, all of it. *And the Beloved came, consumed me, at last.*"

She quietly cried, unable to put her experience into further words.

Exhausted, we slumped down together for warmth and comfort. We rested and even dozed a little. We slept with an arm or hand touching the other, drawing comfort from the physical contact.

During the restless slumber, I had a lucid dream—a dream so powerful that it didn't fade into oblivion later when I awoke.

I was in a small country town and seemed to be watching a long procession of firefighters as they drove their dusty vehicles—fire trucks, small bulldozers and heavy equipment—back from what seemed to have been a long battle with a persistent fire. They looked exhausted but I sensed they had, at last, put the fire out.

Because I saw them park the trucks and begin to congregate in a large field—perhaps to have a follow-up meeting or to receive thanks from their commander—I drove my car up under the trees that encircled the field to try to hear what they were saying.

Another car was beside me and I saw a man outside of it leaning against the hood watching the firemen too.

The man turned to me and I realized it was my <u>father</u> and he looked handsome and in his prime.

Even in my dream, I was aware that he had died several years ago and marveled that I could see his precious face looking at me. I could actually gaze at him fully—taking in every aspect of his presence. But the most glorious thing was… he looked back at me with a happy face, a face that glowed with love and quiet peace. I knew he saw me—all of me, my life, my soul—and he adored me absolutely. He knew everything and, from his perspective, it was all good. All was in Divine order—my life, the firemen and the world.

As I woke much later from the oblivion of sleep, I recognized a strong emotion of joy in my body. *Joy? Why a feeling of joy when we're still trapped in this cave?* I lay there on the dusty floor and then the memory of the dream came rushing back. *"Oh my God… my God."* I basked in the experience of the dream and eventually, the joy seemed to replace what, for so many years, had felt like a void in my soul. Sometime later, I also realized that my father, the former fire-chief, was still watching over his firemen. Perhaps he whispered warnings in their ears and was their guardian angel.

Thoughts swirled in my head about how souls can still be with us after their physical death. For a while I savored the dream experience of my father and eventually told Rachael and Medina about it. The dream reminded me of a true story about one of my dearest friends in the world, Joyce. We called her… Joyous.

Joyous

I told the story.

"Joyous had to live through losing her twenty-five year old daughter to cancer, a daughter who left three babies behind. That very spiritual, religious woman prayed unceasingly for her daughter's life, but she died anyway.

"Joyous dropped into a spiritual crater. When she emerged, she said she couldn't believe in a male theistic God anymore, one that she had to beg for favors.

"*A Presence, a Love,* had been with her, holding her, in her pit of despair. In the dark night of her soul, It told her to get up off her knees and said, 'You are my precious daughter. As part of Me, envision what you want in your life and I will be there. You can create with Me, what you desire. But,' It cautioned, 'be careful with your creative power, precious one. If you worry and obsess about what you <u>don't</u> want, your fears will become real—you will create what you worry about.'

"So, she became a co-creator. She said, 'Whatever happens, ultimately, I know that I will be all right.' Her prayers were, 'Thank You, God.'

"Joyous came out absolutely loving and cherishing life. She said, 'Life *itself* is Holy.' With a beautiful singing voice she sang passionate songs in church, and loved to go dancing.

"She met and married a man who traveled with her, danced with her, and sang with her. She told us, 'The closest we humans can come to Divine Love—to actually <u>experience</u> it while here on earth—is in the physical consummation of love between a man and woman. During that act, admiration, adulation, trust and acceptance permeate every cell of their bodies and *they are One.*'

"I think she represented the 'divine cosmic dance' in joyous female form. She used to say, 'I don't plan on dying. You guys can explore life after death all you want; I'm not leaving!'

"But… lymphoma got her. After a horrible year of chemotherapy, she finally crashed and lapsed into a coma. I went to the hospital and just leaned my head over and pressed it next to her bald little head, silently willing her to feel my love.

"In bed that night around three a.m., I was awakened by a crazed mockingbird outside my open window. That bird was singing <u>*twenty separate and joyously loud songs, in the pitch dark!*</u> The absolutely wild joyful singing by a mockingbird in the middle of the night was so unexplainable that I became convinced that it was a sign from Joyous. It occurred to me that she must have died and was using this mockingbird to try to tell me the glories of the other side. A call in the morning revealed her still alive, still in a coma, with all her family around her. I stayed home.

"The next night at one a.m., the same crazed bird sang loudly and just as exuberantly but from further away, across my little pond. That next day, Joyous died.

"No more mockingbird song after that. No mockingbirds even visited my home, although I searched the trees for weeks. I came to believe that the soul is able to leave a dying body, and somehow she talked that bird into singing at my window. She wanted to tell me what she was finding! It must have been that unfathomable Love that Sonya talked about. Joyous loved me enough to try to tell me what she had found, even in her death. She could at last actually *see* the Divine in all of us, in all of creation—that nature *herself* is the body of God.

"She and Sonya are both gone now, after giving me so much. That's what *I* want to be able to do! To *see*, as God sees, the Divine in everything, even in myself! I want to know enough to give like that, to love like that; to be an example—not to preach—just live!" Both hands went to my heart and I pleaded, "God, I want to *live* to *do* that!"

In that dark cave, my friends came close, touched me, patted me, hugged me and we eventually lay down and arranged ourselves to sleep, tucked together.

It was my turn to be in the middle—the warm space— nurtured by the love surrounding me.

Rachael's prayer came softly. "Baruch Hashem—Blessed be God." She was silent and then spoke again, "You know... there's really nothing *but* God. We are safe, no matter what happens... Gamzuletova. *This, also,* should be for good."

Medina breathed, almost imperceptibly, from behind my ear... "Al *lah,* Al *lah,* Al *lah.*"

All of our paths were leading to Love. Our belief was open-ended. We instinctively knew we were heard... and Loved.

I thought, *At some point, we have to stop talking about God, stop reading our precious books about God, stop our various spiritual practices, and just be still. The stillness is where God has been waiting quietly, patiently for us to come close enough—to touch us—to bring us Home.*

BUDDHISM *"You men are all my children and I am your Father. For age upon age, you have been scorched by multitudinous woes, and I have saved you all."*

Lotus Sutra 3

---

21 Rescue

After three days, the rescuers broke through but the tunnel was so small! It had been decided that we would be swaddled in some slick material and pulled through.

Medina had claustrophobia and dreaded to cover her face with anything.

Rachael, the most voluptuous of us, hoped that her breasts would fit. She knelt down, felt the new space, and wasn't at all sure it would work.

By the next morning, the rescuers had completed necessary preparations. In addition to a flashlight, in came a tube containing an oilcloth sack for each of us to step into for rescue. It had been fashioned into a long bag with the retrieval rope at the head. Two of us would help the first woman in and secure the opening with the side straps attached to the rope. We would knot the straps and yell "Go."

I thought that in case someone got stuck, there should be a rope attached to *our* end of the bag and the skinniest one should be last. That was Medina, so that didn't work. She couldn't stand to cover her own face. So, I decided to be last.

"Hey guys!" I yelled to those at the other end of the tunnel. "This is Jo in here. I think we need an extra strap on the bottom of the bag in case someone gets stuck and we have to pull her back this way. Rachel will be first, then Medina, and I'll be last."

The bag went back out for remodeling to include a thick strap at the bottom for us to use if necessary. We waited impatiently for the ordeal to be over. But, at least, they sent us a little food.

We could hear the sounds of the people outside through the short, open tunnel. Even the smell of the sweaty working men wafted in on a draft of air occasionally. So close!

Finally, the remodeled bag slid back in to us. We pulled it out of its tube and inspected the new strap attached to its bottom. Yanking hard on it, we decided it was, in fact, very sturdy.

At last all was ready.

Rachael went first in case it took two of us to "unstop the plug" that we hoped she wouldn't create. We tried to help her wiggle into the slippery tube of cloth but she wouldn't fit! When they designed the size of the bag, Rachael's breasts were forgotten. We briefly considered asking for a larger bag but Rachael said, "No! Get me in this thing!" So we proceeded to stuff her in like a sausage.

Then, we yelled "Ready?"

The rescuers outside returned "We're ready, here!"

Because of the lack of air inside the bag, we waited 'til the last moment to tie the knot on top and then yelled "Go!"

Happily, Rachael slid right out like a 'greased pig' (such an inappropriate term for a Jewish lady who would *never* touch pork). Everyone roared with joy at the success of the first rescue. It actually worked!

We heard later that it took three people to get Rachael out of the skin-tight bag—one at the foot to hold the bag, using our strap, and two pulling on her arms at the top.

Next went Medina, not quite so nervous after having seen how swift the exit really was. There was a moment—when I closed her up and knotted the top—that she started to panic, but it was over before it turned into a full blown freak-out. Quickly, the outsiders peeled her out almost like a banana.

Then there was just me left.

After stepping into the sack, I wrestled with a way to knot the straps—to close the top of the bag—from *inside* the bag. Anxiety swelled to near panic as I realized that I couldn't use the outside straps. Inside the oil-cloth bag, sweat poured off my body. I stretched my neck and face out to breathe the cave air while the flopping mouth of the sack covered my face. Calling out I said, "Hey guys, I need a minute to figure out how to close this bag." After taking great gulps of air, I pulled the loose top of that airtight bag into a clump inside, trying to hold the stiff material closed with my clenched fists. It was awkward but would probably work. Scrambling to open it back up, I sucked in the cave air with gratitude.

"Ok, guys. I'm just about ready. I'll yell 'Go', alright?"

"We're ready. Just yell."

I took more deep breaths and whispered, "Into Your hands I commend my spirit." Then, slipping down inside, I grabbed that awkward wad of cloth with a death grip. That sucker was all bunched up in front of my face as I yelled "Go!"

Nothing happened… "Go!" I screamed again… no movement… *They couldn't hear me through the thick cloth!* I burst back out the opening and yelled, "Just a minute! I have to leave an opening in this sack so you'll be able to *hear* me. Get ready again, ok?"

"Okay, we're ready out here."

So I went back into my claustrophobic sack and after bunching it back closed, carefully loosened a hole and screamed with all my might, "Go!"

As it turned out, the bag slid off one shoulder anyway, and rocks scraped at me. But, *I was coming out of there,* even if I lost parts of myself along the way!

In just moments, I was so grateful for the man with strong arms that scooped me out of the "shroud" and lifted my whole body onto a waiting stretcher. I was rolled down the cave corridor and out into the sunshine.

Blinding light and screaming bedlam assaulted my senses. I felt totally disoriented! Multitudes of people were pressed all around me, yelling wildly at the successful rescue. I couldn't see anything because of the sun's painful glare in my eyes...

As I was rolled up to two transport vehicles that sat in the shade, they looked like elongated golf carts with the back seats removed. When I tried to climb down from the stretcher and get into the cart, I realized that all the starch was gone from my body. My legs wobbled and again, the strong, steadying arms of a nameless angel helped me onto a tiny cot in the golf cart.

There was Rachael beside me on *her* cot, giggling!

"Rachael, what is so funny?" I was wiped out and she was laughing?

She chuckled, "I finally got that *golf cart* I wanted when we started this fiasco!"

The laughter helped to recharge me and we happily jiggled and bumped along the narrow jungle path back to civilization.

"At least it isn't a donkey," I added.

We women were whisked up and driven straight to the hospital to be checked out thoroughly. My shoulder was cleaned and dressed with antibiotic ointment. Hungry, exhausted and grateful, we got to shower and donned clean clothes some thoughtful person had retrieved from our rooms. Food and drinks arrived, and were ravenously consumed.

Jack was there to greet us with Miguel, John and the whole troupe, as we walked out to the bus to go back to the hotel.

It was bittersweet without Sonya.

---

22 *Jack*

After the rescue, Jack had waited impatiently during their emergency room visit, to speak to the women—especially Jo. But then, all he got was public hugging all around as they were boarding their bus to the hotel.

While he waited, he rehashed and rehashed the cave-in tragedy. That fatal day, outside of the cave, the ground slightly trembled with a small earthquake, while inside the cave, hell broke loose. After frantically counting heads, he had realized that Sonya, Jo, Medina and Rachael were missing—in there! Todd and Takil had barely made it out just as the ceiling collapsed.

Miguel had immediately alerted the authorities to action and the call for help went out.

Jack had paced back and forth—unable to even sit down— and grumbled under his breath, "Why are they so slow? Damned Mexicans!"

Miguel stepped just inside the cave entrance and listened carefully. He came running back out to say, "I think I heard some noises coming from the other side of the cave-in."

Disregarding the danger, Jack had walked down into the cave to the blockade and yelled loudly, "Sonya? Jo?"

Then he had waited... nothing... then called again... and—yes—mumbled sounds were there! Maybe they were all safe, just trapped. Excited, he had raced out to tell everyone. They were—all four of the women—*his charges!* This had happened on his watch. Guilt and tears had overcome him and he stomped into the jungle to hide.

He had thought, *Why did I listen to the advice of the hotel manager and change my itinerary to include the cave? It was all my fault! If only I had been more careful, hadn't broken my own tour rules and led them to a site I hadn't personally inspected. I put them in harm's way.*

Standing in the jungle that day, the gray sky had opened up and cold raindrops pounded his head and shoulders. He had thought, *It serves you right Jack Zuko! Take your punishment!*

His mind had started making desperate plans, bargains with God. *If Jo's alive, I'll sweep her off her feet and marry her and take her with me on my trips. Please God, let her be alive.*

Now that he *knew* she was alive, his heart spoke in an undeniable voice, *No Jack, your wander-lusting ways will slowly kill her if you try to take her for your own.* A sinking in his chest validated the voice. He couldn't change—didn't really want to change. But Jo was so vital, so alive and precious.

The Mexican rescue team had really arrived quickly, worked out their plans, and started bringing in equipment to drill a tunnel to the interior. *But it had been so hard to wait.*

Then, with a great sigh of relief, "Oh God… they're safe—they're out… … … except for Sonya…"

When the three women had each emerged from the cave, one by one, his huge fear had gradually dissolved, leaving a small ache in his heart for Sonya. *Oh Lord… Sonya…*

I have to see Jo—but she needs rest. Maybe by lunch time…

TAOISM *"Thus it is that the TAO produces (all things), nourishes them, brings them to their full growth, nurses them, completes them, matures them, maintains them, and over-spreads them."*

The Tao-te Ching (Lao-tzu)

---

23 Jo

My hotel room looked like heaven. Full of thanksgiving, I crawled between those immaculate sweet-smelling sheets and sank into oblivion.

Jack called my room several hours later to ask if we could get together to talk. I was hungry again, so I met him in the hotel restaurant. We slid into a booth sitting opposite each other. The food arrived quickly, but Jack didn't start eating as I attacked my loaded plate.

When my eating slowed enough that he had a chance, he grasped one of my hands and confessed how guilty he felt for the whole disaster. "I made the change of plans to include that cave and caused it all—putting everyone in danger."

I put down my fork and held both of his hands. Looking straight into his guilty eyes, I said, "I feel like it was just in the cards—perhaps our destiny."

His red, tormented face blanched with shock as his eyes widened and his jaw went slack.

"Sonya was complete," I said. "The night before the cave-in, she expressed to me that she was content with the life she had lived. It felt complete. And now I feel that each of us, we three surviving women, needed that calamity to push us forward in our own soul growth."

My throat closed due to unexpressed tears. Finally able to speak, I scrambled to find the words to explain the unexplainable. "I think we all agreed, on some higher level, to go through that horror. When we were in the cave, our stone prison was a sort of incubator. It forced us to just <u>be</u> in that place. I had time to evaluate my life—to actually see what a magnificent process it has been. Each bump in my road heralded a growth spurt that I could finally appreciate.

"The poet Rumi believed we have to be 'burned by the Beloved'— by the divine experience of being human—to really truly 'get it'. My fellow cave-mates were also transforming—a metamorphosis was happening. We stood as midwives to each other—witnessed the birth, the miracle of new spiritual understanding as it grew in each one of us.

"We have been indelibly changed forever and I think the full understanding, the impact of that metamorphosis will keep coming, will keep revealing itself over the weeks and months to come.

"Jack, you were only the catalyst, the tool God used to make it happen. Why do you think you broke your own tour rules and impulsively added that cave for us to enjoy? You were nudged into it by your inner voice."

I looked at him to see how my words were being received.

He sat very still—looking at me with such love, such respect—such *relief.* Tears threatened to spill out of his eyes, so he gruffly grabbed his napkin and examined the cold food.

After a few moments, we realized that the cold enchiladas were not very appetizing. Jack called the waiter and ordered another round of the same, so we could enjoy them hot.

While we waited for the food, he said, "Jo, I was in agony thinking that you had been killed in the cave and so happy to see your dirt-covered smile erupt from that escape sack."

I giggled and said, "I don't know what I expected to see in the mirror at the hospital but it was *not* a raccoon lady looking back at me, thanks to all the tears and dust. What a shock."

"You were a grubby but unbelievably precious sight to my eyes," he said. "During the painful wait to see if you survived, all I could think about was to see you again. Then when you were rescued, reality set in." He stopped speaking.

Jack drew in a deep breath, blew it out and admitted, "I've had the honor of being loved by two incredible women in my life. The first was my wife, for ten years. The second was a long-term relationship a few years after my divorce. Those two women were the best things that ever happened to me, but I killed their love with neglect, because I absolutely obsess about the work I do. I crave to get on the road as much as possible—to explore the world and meet new exciting people. That obsession always won out over my relationships." He hung his head and admitted, "There's a high I get from being the expert and receiving all that admiration."

I thought, *Oh Jack, you are finally opening up to me. At last, you are giving me the part of you I wanted all along.*

He leaned on the table and looked tenderly into my eyes. "I'm just beginning to see how exceptional you are, the depth of you." He grinned devilishly as he said, "I was blinded by your saucy red-headed body and the challenge in your eyes. I wanted you badly, and now even more. You would be *so easy* to love. But I realize now that you deserve more... A woman like you deserves a full time man and lover. Losing you is preferable to selfishly taking you for my own, but not being able to do you justice—to give you what you need."

We sat there in silence, smiling into each other's eyes and anticipating the loss.

I got up and slid into Jack's side of the booth and admitted, "You're a very enticing man, Jack Zuko. I *almost* love you already." The thought about how his mouth tasted, popped into my mind. He somehow got that message and leaned over to kiss me softly, thoroughly, deliciously. When my mind recovered it said, *You have wanted him because he's so unavailable, ultimately.*

The fresh food arrived right at that moment and I wondered if the waiter saw us and paused with his delivery until the timing was better. He did leave the table with a smirk on his face. *Oh well...*

The spicy enchiladas disappeared quite rapidly this time. Sitting close beside Jack in the booth, the discussion moved to the loss of Sonya. The ache of our shared grief caused me to lean into him. As he leaned back into me, our lowered heads touched. It seemed right, so we just kept them together and held her, our beloved Sonya, between us.

In a bit, we talked and even laughed a little about memorable events of the trip. I realized exhaustion was oozing out of my bones so we hugged each other one more time and Jack leaned back to look at me, an open invitation in his eyes. I was tempted. *Oh Man! Was I tempted,* but the exhaustion won out and the moment passed. We parted and went back, each to our own room.

Who Am I?

Late that night in bed, I thought about all that had happened on this long trip and the upcoming return home. I wondered, *who is this person that will be going home?* Most people define themselves by the content of their lives, and I had done that, up to this point. While I comfortably reclined against the bed pillows, I once more scrutinized my life and all I had accomplished. Satisfied that it was a pretty good record over all, I then realized that being alone did have some benefits. I had actually come to *like* myself and that was more than sufficient.

My eye fell on the Mayan astrology birthday book that Jack had passed out. Its corner was hanging out of my suitcase. I scrambled off the bed and retrieved it, curious about my birthdate information.

My sign was Ahau, my planet was Pluto, and my birthright— my purpose this time—was Divine Love personified on Earth. My energy number was 13, the energy that encompasses all of the other energies. Pluto symbolizes the *warrior* who may not use methods of war to confront negative energies, but is allowed only to protect with steadfast courage and to teach by example.

How could I live up to that reading? I vowed to clean up my act and strive for perfection, like Rachael.

*But then I heard Sonya's voice in my mind, "You don't have to strive at all. You just have to **be**! Just be in the Presence and all things will come to you."*

Now, I sensed my own presence, my naked, unveiled, unclothed *being-ness.* It was untouched by young or old, rich or poor, good or bad, or any other attributes. And I wasn't *alone.* There, nestled among the pillows, I was embraced by Love. My shoulders felt covered with warmth, as if a down comforter had fallen over them.

The *gift* of the cave was to crystallize the course—the trajectory of my life. I was headed back to the Loving Oneness from which we all came.

I silently prayed and thanked God for providing the next right step. Enveloped in the experience of God, I sat in meditation for a long time and had a vision that changed my life.

My Vision

I was a point of light, a spark, floating with many other points of light in a twilight sea. I was drifting onto a low flat beach where the waves were curling up and making lacy patterns on the sand. I knew that we were coming Home, even though all I could see was a twilight land with nothing distinguishable.

We knew it was Home and we could feel the multitudes of spirits there, celebrating our return and honoring us for being <u>brave</u> enough to get into a body and experience the exhilarations and devastations of an Earthly life. We each had been to war and were rolling up on a beach like Normandy but... coming to Peace.

*Each was so proud to have done it! We understood that it ultimately <u>didn't matter</u> how <u>well</u> we had done it, only that **we** <u>had done it!</u>*

Sonya's Book

Lots of good food and restful sleep in clean soft beds gave the 'cave women' renewed energy, but the tragedy of the cave left us somewhat subdued. No one else really wanted to do the last Mayan ruin site either, so it was agreed to end the tour. Everyone started to make plans to leave.

The rescuers now concentrated on retrieving Sonya's body.

Her family called me long distance, hoping that I would stay and oversee the cremation arrangements they had made. Her ashes were to be flown home along with her suitcase and clothes, which I would pack.

Sonya had talked with them a few days before the tragedy and said how much she had "grown to love Jo and depend on her". So, they asked if I would accept a gift of the hummingbird pendant that Sonya had purchased while we were together in Peru.

"I would love to have it," I said appreciatively.

Sonya's daughter then asked another favor, "Rachael has been helping Mother with her book. They agreed that it was done—finally finished."

"What... done?" I couldn't comprehend that.

"Yes, it's a small book and they felt that it was complete. Could you give mother's laptop to Rachael so she can print out copies of the book to give your tour members as a parting gift from my mother?"

"I'll get it right to her." While I was grateful that Sonya's book would live on after her death, my heart contracted with the pain of having been excluded from her writing. It still hurt.

The ever-efficient Rachael made the miracle happen and the gift of Sonya's book, encased in a pretty red folder, was showered on our troupe members and guides.

That night a beautiful farewell dinner was held around the hotel's moonlit pool, surrounded by fragrant plants and flowers. The flames of lanterns nodded gently in the night breeze. Sonya's wonderful little book was the main topic of conversation. Everyone spoke excitedly about her wisdom and talent and applauded Rachael for her efforts at printing it out.

Home and email addresses were exchanged by all and another book was handed out with pictures of all of us and the various guides. Sonya was there between the pages.

In misery, I went to sit in a chair by myself on the edge of the patio, next to some aromatic flowering shrubs. My ego was hemorrhaging. Trying to bind the wound, I attempted to reason away the pain in my heart that had been reopened with Sonya's book celebration. The book was small and I had read it. It *was* good. Sonya's wisdom and unconditional love colored every page.

*Only I had been excluded from that love because I told her the introduction (her short biographical story) was **boring**, while the rest of* *the book was written so well. And then I had said that rude word again,* <u>boring</u>*! I still flinched at the memory of the cold silent stare she gave me as she abruptly closed the computer and cut me out of that part of her heart from then on. I noticed that she eventually re-wrote it beautifully, just as I suggested, but the damage was done. Oh, why couldn't she have excused my rudeness, forgiven me? Now, it was too late. I could never make it up to her.*

Feelings of not being good enough—being flawed—rolled over me in waves. Senseless anger boiled out of my heart, directed at her and myself. I felt like a worm, speared with a fish hook, flailing ineffectually around—doomed.

All the while, the party swirled around me. Someone placed a plate of food in front of me. It went unnoticed.

This is insanity! It's all totally unimportant, inconsequential! Why am I so upset? Why can't I reason it away? How can I be all spiritual one day, and a completely screwed up human being the next? Leaning my head back on the chair, I breathed in deeply, taking in the fragrance of flowers around me, one slow breath at a time. I sucked in my pain, down into my wounded heart, and tried to blow out love.

It didn't work. Out of desperation I mentally got on my knees and begged, *Please take this pain away Lord—I can't fix it! Take it from me.* Sitting silently beside the pool, I was oblivious to my happy comrades as they moved noisily around me.

A voice in my head said, as if to others with it, *"Okay, it is healed."* My eyes popped open; my consciousness returned to the party. My heart was calm... no pain. When called upon, God answered with a miracle, *again*. The anguish was completely gone, never to return.

Medina and Rachael gently slipped into chairs at my side and patted my hand. They didn't know what had been going on with me but suspected it was grief for Sonya. They were right.

As the three of us huddled together once again, we were almost completely surrounded by deliciously scented flowering shrubs. A whirring sound came from the bushes and then a tiny hummingbird flew right up to my nose and hovered there. I peered into its face in disbelief. *I'm not wearing the red that usually attracts them and hummingbirds don't fly after dark.*

Delighted, I carefully motioned for Rachael and Medina to look. Holding our breath, we watched it fly in and out and all around us. Then it streaked across the pool and buzzed so close to Jack's ear that he flinched instinctively, trying to bat it away but, thankfully, too late.

We broke out into sudden laughter and tears. It had to be Sonya, saying "Goodbye."

The heartwarming encounter with the hummingbird left me feeling loved... and forgiven.

To embody unconditional love had been my ultimate goal for a long time. Because of Sonya and her love (and *my perception* of her withdrawal of that love) the responsibility involved in personifying *unconditional* love dawned on me. You can never take it back, once offered. *Conditional* love can be a lethal weapon, capable of cutting a person down faster than a sword.

This Dance

As the party seemed to be winding down, we heard the sound of big wooden glass doors being pushed open to expose the hotel bar. Lively Mexican music poured out into the open air, seeming to revive us.

We watched and listened as a Flamenco guitarist strolled out to us, bringing heightened emotions on his twelve strings. When his song was finished, Jack went to him and bent his head in a shared conversation.

The guitar player nodded enthusiastically and began to strum a Tango! Softly, a horn moaned accompaniment from the bar.

Jack came to me and bowed. Then his eyes searched my face with longing as he lifted his hand, imploring me to dance.

Our troupe stood silently, at attention. A few curious faces peered out from the bar.

I rose, amid scattered applause, and he led me to the wide space encircling the pool. We walked side by side in the Tango walk, exhibiting a studied, hyper-consciousness of each measured step.

Our Tango would eventually take a counter-clockwise path, all the way around the pool.

As we arrived at the wide space where we would begin the actual dance, Jack's arm came out and encircled my back with intensity, as if we were beginning the final 'dance of our life.'

The flamenco guitar pulled emotions from us, enlivened and drove us to our task. At one with the music, at one with life and at one with each other, we carefully placed steps of intense sadness, while accompanied by the mournful, hidden horn. Then, the guitar spun us around with feelings of joy and gratitude, and throughout the dance, we brushed against each other with tender affection.

Once, I instinctively lifted my hand and caressed his head as in a blessing, before my fingers dropped down along his sweating neck and rested again, on the muscular shoulder in motion. It was a different Tango, this one, but even more powerful for all that we had lived through; the love, the experience-based knowledge, and the sadness of tragedy. The Tango was a fitting end to the tour and heralded the end of our relationship. It was over and we both knew it. We made love with our Tango, for all to see.

Applause from the small crowd filled the air as our dance ended. We bowed, smiling in response.

Jack squeezed my hand, one last time, and then went to congratulate the guitarist.

Mildred appeared at my shoulder, her face glistening with tears. "Oh sister... Life sure bruises the heart, don't it?"

Quick tears filled my own eyes in response to her compassion. "Yes... Yes it does." I reached out and hugged her to me. My sister. "But the bruising causes a softening, don't you think?"

She pulled back and smiled through her tears. "That's the point, I guess. *My* heart won't ever be the same after this tour."

We nodded to each other. "Yes... Yes..."

When it was time to go up to bed, I glanced over at Jack. Thoroughly enjoying himself, he circled through the happy tour group; he was laughing, joking and appreciating each one—bidding each individual a personal goodbye.

As if he knew I was watching him, he stopped to look at me. A brief expression of longing was quickly eclipsed by a warm smile that spread across his face. He bowed his head and then looked back at me as if to acknowledge the whole of our relationship with gratitude.

While mentally kissing him goodbye, and full of regret for what might have been, I realized the hole in my soul was filled. I wasn't driven toward this unavailable man anymore, to get my life lesson. That was over too—completed.

But I thought of our Tango, the first glorious Tango with Jack. *That* was a highlight of my life and I would be eternally grateful. I had *so* wanted to dance, but I was scared of failure. First, I got the correct teacher, who worked at the Tango club. That man helped me to remember the steps. Then, the real passion for the dance began with Jack—the perfect partner to teach the next steps... of love. Oh...

the splendor and the agony of trying to get that Tango right—those dueling emotions of anguish and attraction—the moving away and the coming near again.

Our dance is finished—Jack and I. But, I saw that the dance of life was also ahead of me and I knew I was ready, brave enough to dance again.

I realized, *It's all about relationships—this dance! This Love that I'm after can be found in other relationships too, with a lover, a father, a child, a friend, an adversary when reconciled, Mother Nature, an intimate relationship with God... and especially, with our Self.*

Acknowledgements

Many of the stories in this book are thanks to a memorable South American tour, made possible by my precious Aunt Jo Audas. Even in her early 80's, she was a lively and enthusiastic traveling partner as we journeyed together.

Eternal thanks goes to my friend, Lynn Hopkins. She patiently examined and edited every word of my stories, over and over, as I continued to change the text and yet she faithfully preserved my "voice". During the process, she taught me some of the intricacies of writing and the power of punctuation. Her gift for more authentic dialogue was valuable. Lynn's was a labor of love, and I'm so grateful, especially for the times she stubbornly held her ground, like a bulldog, and consequently, forced me to write a better book.

Thanks also goes to my literary and gardening friend, Kathy Wagenknecht, an author of several enjoyable books. She kindly gave me a reality check and sound advice when I proudly handed her my very ragged first draft.

Thankfulness is due to my dear friend, Diane Butturff. She graciously and lovingly shared her perspective and personal knowledge of Hassidic Judaism and the Kabbalah.

Appreciation is also due to my newest friend, Sophia Said, to whom I reached out and found insider's knowledge, told by a woman born and raised in Pakistan. She is a woman who has fully embraced life in the United States and, at the same time, she is helping us to really understand and appreciate her beautiful Islamic faith and culture. She is the inspiration for my fictional character, Medina.

I am indebted to Huston Smith's books, *The World's Religions* and *A Seat at the Table*. I studied and used them like text books.

I am grateful to my friend and author of many books, Jim Young, who wrote the book *2013: The Beginning is Here*. In that book, he introduced me to the work of Dr. José A. Arguelles and his book, *The Mayan Factor: Path Beyond Technology*. Also in the book *2013*, Jim had a chapter by Miguel Angel Vergara. He is man I had grown to know and admire while in Mexico participating in his Mayan Tour group. I was reminded of his teachings and then researched them on Miguel's website for more information on which to base my fictional character of Miguel.

Also, I owe much gratitude to Dolores Cannon, an author and regression hypnotherapist. I have grown immensely through reading so many of her books and attending her Transformation Conferences. It was actually at one of those conferences that I first began to piece together the concepts that enabled me to write this book.

The Near Death Experience as told on YouTube by Anita Moorjani ultimately remodeled my concept of life after death, and became the pattern of the NDE experienced by my character Sonya. Anita subsequently wrote the book, *Dying to be Me.*

One of my most sustaining spiritual sources is the magazine *Science of Mind—A Guide for Spiritual Living.* Earnest Holmes was the founder of the Religious Science Movement and this periodical. I am most grateful for this avenue of spiritual inspiration. (His Church of Religious Science should not be confused with the Church of Scientology, a separate entity.)

Much gratitude is due to Don Meyers whose technical and artistic assistance was needed to turn my pastel painting into a beautifully lettered and proportioned cover.

My daughter, Melissa Sorrells, turned out to be a most valued asset toward the end of this literary adventure. Her editing support was a gift I had not expected.

And last, but most importantly, I would like to thank my husband Don who has been my rock and beloved partner in creating a life and family together. He has also been exceedingly patient in dealing with my spotty presence during the writing of this book.

About the Author

Alice Holeman lives in Little Rock, Arkansas with her husband and a large busy family. She is a retired Registered Nurse and a watercolor artist. A lifetime passion for nature has fostered expressions that include creating gardens of rocks, plants and waterfalls. Writing is her newest creative media and passion and the cover for *Life is a Tango* is her own illustration.

Journaling, meditation, studying, and an active church life nurture her walk with the Beloved.